KNOCK KNOCK

Equestrian Fiction by Barbara Morgenroth

BITTERSWEET FARM 13

KNOCK KNOCK

Barbara Morgenroth

DashingBooks

Bittersweet Farm 13: Knock Knock © 2016
Barbara Morgenroth
http://barbaramorgenroth.com

This is a work of fiction. While references may be made to actual places or events, all names, characters, incidents and locations are from the author's imagination and do not resemble any actual living or dead persons, businesses, or events.

Any similarity is coincidental.

ISBN: 978-0692701133

Cover photo by Irene Elise Powlick
Published by DashingBooks
Text set in Adobe Garamond

AUGUST

1

WHILE IT WAS IMPOSSIBLE to get lost in our woods,
CB and I tried very hard. We went up the mountain and
down the other side, leaving our property and finally
reaching the end of the dirt road.

This was the kind of trail ride I used to take with Butch
when being home was worse than the deer flies or winter's
cold. I felt alone, although that was far from reality. Jules
would have returned from her shopping trip by now, Greer
was in her office, and my father was in the den. Lockie and
Cam had left before dawn to look for a couple horses. Even
though he didn't tell me, I knew they were going to the
track. I wasn't opposed to rescuing racehorses, just
disturbed we couldn't rescue all of them.

My phone rang and I dug it out of my pocket.

"Hi."

"Where are you?" Greer asked.

"On the road, I'll be home in a few minutes. Why?"

"A family meeting has been called about the lawsuit."

"You can tell me about it," I replied.

The last thing I wanted to hear about was Paul Gish suing me because his daughter, Ami, had fallen off at a horse show when she wasn't even my student at the time. The way she rode, I would have had her in Pet Pony until she could keep her legs on the saddle. She certainly had no business jumping anything higher than a pole on the ground.

The only way I could explain it to myself was that Paul was in a very competitive field, show business, and expected his daughter to shine whether she wanted to or not. No one at the farm had the sense that Ami enjoyed horses or riding, yet she was taking lessons.

Maybe it would have been good publicity for Paul or if Ami had been successful, it would have brought him into proximity of important people. Perhaps all he wanted was a job. Or he wanted to brag "That's my daughter. She won a championship."

I understood how it could be embarrassing for Paul to push Ami so hard and have her spend the rest of the summer in a cast. None of it seemed like her idea, but it could have been. At her exclusive school, being a winning rider would be a real benefit to her social life.

That's how I always felt when I was attending The Briar School. There were girls who won at nearly everything and then there were the rest of us losers.

Every time I went through town and drove past the school, I was thankful I didn't have to put up with that nonsense any longer.

"Talia," Greer said. "This is important."

"Isn't it all going to happen without me?"

CB turned down the driveway without any input from me.

"You can't pretend it's not happening."

"That's not what I'm doing. It's a frivolous lawsuit that Paul Gish can't win and he's going to talk trash about me for the next year."

"That changes nothing. I'll be at the house." Greer clicked off.

I stroked CB's neck as we approached the barn. "Thank you for being good company."

He stopped; I slid off, and then brought him into the barn.

"Everyone's looking for you," Cap said as she picked out the stalls before lunch.

"I'm in no great rush to hear about the lawsuit. Everyone in the county will know."

"Not everyone," Cap pointed out too reasonably.

"I enjoy being anonymous. People like to talk about other people. I don't want to be the object of their derision."

Cap paused at the manure wagon. "Do you think that the students at the school I hadn't even begun to attend didn't find my situation hilarious?"

I clipped CB to the crossties. "I didn't really think about it."

"Of course not. People have their own issues on their minds. There are always mean girls who enjoy seeing someone humiliated."

"I'm sorry."

I was. I knew Cap had gone through an embarrassing experience with her father but she was right. To me, it was in the past and hadn't seemed important.

"This is nothing. My father was on television and interviewed in magazines. Then there was the television movie. For three years it didn't stop."

"Who knew you could break the law and become a celebrity by doing so?"

"We're lucky he didn't become a reality TV star."

I glanced over to see if she was kidding. She wasn't.

"You've had a tough time," I said.

"There were a couple bumps in the road but nothing major. Neither is your lawsuit. Just don't post any spicy photos on the internet and this will be forgotten when the next fake scandal hits. People without lives of their own have to talk about someone else. It's just entertainment."

"Ruining my reputation shouldn't be entertainment."

"Stop being so dramatic. Greg trashed his reputation, but he has a job, and is still training horses. In another six months, trust me, no one will remember what he did."

As I put CB in his stall, I heard a truck pull into the yard. At first, I thought it might be Lockie, but then realized it didn't sound like his truck.

By the time Cap and I reached the doorway, a young woman was getting out of her truck.

"Hi. I was told to ask for Talia."

"That's me."

She smiled as she approached us. "I'm Dina Gnehmn. You might have a pony going by the name Penuche."

"We sure do," I replied.

"He was my first show pony. I adored him but then I outgrew him and we couldn't keep two horses. I've been searching for him ever since I graduated from college and got my own barn."

"Come on, he's inside right now," I said and started for the lower barn.

"This is not the only Penuche I've tracked down," Dina told me.

"Other people were crazy enough to name a pony after a hard to spell and pronounce candy?"

"Yes. He was Mister Twister to me."

5

"We call him Oh Fudge," Cap said.

"He's a lesson pony?"

"Yes, but not in that way. He's ridden about five times a week."

"Five days?" she asked, concerned.

I knew she was imagining that the pony was being ridden into the ground. "No, just five times. He's in perfect health, sound and happy."

"This is like a horse resort," Cap said as we went through the barn. "Humans are the only ones who work their butts off."

I stopped at his stall where Fudge was eating his lunchtime hay.

"Twisty?"

His head rose immediately.

"May I go in?" Dina asked.

"Of course. Take your time and kiss him all you want," I said, opening the stall door.

Cap and I left the barn.

"It would have been better if he hadn't pooped immediately after he came in.

"They're reverse house-broken, if you never noticed," I replied as we sat at the picnic table to wait for Dina.

That weekend, Cap was scheduled to ride Spare in the pre-green jumper division at a show Cam was attending over the weekend. They had been working together when he had a chance, and thought she was ready. With room on the Acadiana trailer, she was going.

We talked about that since Cap had never been to any of the larger shows with Bijou. She had groomed for Cam and Lockie enough times that nothing should come as a surprise. With Cam looking out for her, I wasn't worried.

"I expect nothing," she said. "There will be so many professionals riding in the classes, this really is just for experience."

"That's the best way to look at it. None of the jumps will be bigger than anything you've ridden at home."

"I'm more concerned with the noise and activity being a distraction."

"That's the experience part. We could bring him to the County Fair and let him stand around being bored for a couple hours."

"Good idea," Cap agreed.

Dina walked up to the picnic table and sat across from us. I could see that she had been crying.

"How much do you want for him?"

"The promise if you ever need to let him go, you'll bring him back here."

"He'll be with me forever."

"Then I guess you're set."

"You must want some money." She took out a checkbook. "I can give you a down payment and make arrangements for later."

"That's not necessary. Fudge, Twisty," I corrected myself, "was given to me. You don't need to pay me for him."

"I could pay the person who gave him to you."

"That's a very nice gesture, but we'll just consider it even, and that no one owes anyone anything."

"Thank you. Do you mind if I hang around today?"

"Not at all. Where's home?"

"Northern Virginia."

"Will you be back tomorrow?"

"I'll have someone meet me here. Is there any place to stay overnight?"

"The Inn," Cap and I said simultaneously.

"It's very nice. I'm sure you'll be comfortable," I added.

My phone began ringing, so I stood. "I have a family meeting. If you need anything, Cap will be here, and in another hour or so, my pony riders will be arriving. I'm sure you'll find them very entertaining. Tell them about the time you fell off and they'll have a fit of giggles. I love making them laugh."

"Thanks for the tip."

I got into my truck and drove up to the house so Greer wouldn't be any more annoyed with me than she was already.

Everyone was at the kitchen table waiting as I entered.

"Did you get lost between the road and the barn?" Greer asked.

"No. Fudge's person came looking for him so he's going home to Virginia with her tomorrow." I washed my hands at the kitchen sink. "His real name is Mister Twister."

I sat at my place, Lockie's seat empty to one side. "Give it to me straight."

Realizing how hungry I was, I reached for a grilled chicken sandwich and saw the delicate greenery fringing the crust. "Baby watercress. My favorite."

Jules returned my smile, obviously having made the special effort to cheer me up today.

"He's suing us. We're suing him. Let's eat," my father said.

There was sparkling iced tea with orange slices so thin they were nearly transparent, two salads and several choices of sandwiches. For dessert, there tartlettes of rosy peaches on top of sliced almonds and almond pastry cream, scented with sprigs of rosemary.

For a moment, I stopped eating. Then there was the light touch of Jules's hand on my arm.

Overwhelmed, I took a deep breath. This was my family. Minus a few important members.

"When's the last time you rode," I asked her.

"Summer camp when I was eleven."

"Would you like to pick up where you left off?"

"I don't have aspirations as a future Olympian," Jules replied.

"So you could take walks in the woods with us."

"Henry would make a terrific babysitter," Greer said.

"Lockie's show horse?" Jules asked in shock.

"Greer's right," I replied. "He's very quiet. So is Keynote. Or Splashie."

"Right. Roll the Dice practically falls asleep on the hunt field. He's somnambulistic," Greer added.

"Don't let them talk you into anything you don't want to do," my father said. "They've been practicing their manipulation techniques for years."

"Dad!"

"Deadly. It always works on me," he replied and gave me a wink.

"Maybe," Jules said. "It would be hard for me to cook with a broken arm."

"Why would you fall off when the Zuckerlumpens don't?" I asked.

"Talia's a very good teacher," Greer said.

"Thank you."

2

THIS WAS THE FIRST TIME the 4-H riders had come to the barn and we were going to review and restate everything they should know over the next weeks.

Poppy was riding Twisty so Dina could see him go and Gincy was riding Call.

We talked about balance, and how a horse had to adjust for the weight of a rider. No one had ever considered that before. I wasn't surprised. I hadn't given much thought to what Butch had gone through to carry me around the ring at all those shows either. Certainly none of the trainers I'd had mentioned anything so esoteric. These young ladies would be introduced to thinking about riding.

All four were strong but unpolished. They could stay on, but their positions were more like someone preparing to join Teddy Roosevelt and the Rough Riders for a gallop up San Juan Hill. The basics were familiar but they didn't know the why behind anything.

I wasn't worried. Explanations were an easy part of their education and I assigned them homework. Greer and I had looked through all the riding manuals appropriate for their age group and ability, and we had sent for them. When they had made it through this book, if they were still with me, I would get them another book to study. Thinking about horsemanship wasn't enough, it required action. If I was going to stand there and teach them, they had to meet me half way.

We worked on transitions going from a trot to a walk, and a walk back to a trot. This was something I had worked on every session with the Zuckerlumpens to improve their balance and feel as well as keeping their attention focused. Transitioning between gaits and within gaits increased the horse's ability to organize the movements of his body. It was a very simple litmus test to see where the horse and rider were in their training.

I was very pleased with the progress Gincy and Poppy had made in the months we'd been working together. They didn't know more than the new girls did when they arrived, and now they understood.

"Good work, everyone. Cap will help you take care of your ponies and horses. I'll see you next week," I said, and turned to leave the ring.

Dina was beaming at Twisty as she gave him a treat, and thanked Poppy for the excellent ride. After sliding off, Poppy handed her the reins.

Lockie got off his seat on top of the picnic table and walked over to me. "You're a good instructor. Transitions were a good choice."

"I learned from the best," I replied.

"There are many students and few scholars," he replied, taking my hand. "I'm just a student."

"The horses are always teaching but most riders think it's the other way around."

He tugged me closer and kissed my cheek. "We picked up a couple nice prospects and dropped them off at Rowe House. Victoria was not home but Greg was, so Cam and I had a chance to design a program for them."

"Are they horribly underweight?"

"They're racing trim. We'll give them some time off in the pasture to kick back and relax. Then they can be introduced to their new life."

"I hope it's a better life."

"We'll find people who will appreciate them."

We walked toward the house.

"Can you do without me for a couple hours?" Lockie asked as we neared the driveway.

"Yes. Go take a nap. Do you need something to eat?"

"We ate. It was far below Jules's standards."

"Okay. See you later."

He paused. "I'm fine."

"Of course."

We would sustain the little white lie that he was fine and that I believed him.

If Lockie didn't eat regularly, didn't have water, and was in the truck for as many hours as he had been, a headache would be the result. As I entered the kitchen, I decided to check on him in an hour to bring him some electrolytes and food.

"Just the person I wanted to see," Jules said. "What are you doing this weekend?"

"It's the County Fair. I have seven girls riding on Sunday."

"What are you doing on Saturday?"

"What answer are you looking for?" I asked.

"Jules, I'm doing nothing and would love to sit with you for the pie judging contest."

I was baffled. "Why would we go to a pie competition?"

"Because I'm the judge and I would like your company."

"Thank you, but how did you get to be the judge?"

She added some banana, fragrant slices of peach and fresh mint from the garden into the blender, with yogurt and ice, then turned the device on. A moment later, Jules poured it into a large glass and handed it to me.

"No fennel," she assured me.

I sipped the drink. "Delicious."

"Whoever had agreed to be the judge of the pies had to back out so Mrs. Meade suggested me. I know a little about pies."

"You're an expert," I replied.

"You're dear. So, yes?"

"Is it all day or can I oversee the Zuckerlumpens for a few hours?"

"It's just late morning. It starts at ten. We should be home before one if necessary."

"Okay. I'll go. Do we have to eat pie?"

"Yes, we would taste every pie in competition."

"Is it like that wine show we saw, where you taste it and spit it out?"

"Talia!"

"Well..."

"Their feelings would get hurt."

I nodded and finished my smoothie.

***

Cap and Emma were working Available over a gymnastic Lockie had created for Dice who needed a refresher course in everything. There were four poles on the ground. After that the horse was turned either to the right or left to make a large circle with three small jumps

15

equidistant from each other. Bending was an integral part of the exercise, as opposed to so many gymnastics, which were ridden on a straight line.

Ridden in a fat egg-butt snaffle, Available was very handy and able to do everything we'd asked of him so far.

Emma was the kind of rider who seemed to be velcroed onto the horse, a result of riding bareback up and down the hills near her father's California farm. Completely in synch with the motion, Emma never seemed to lose her balance or feel. The problem was that she was less unaccustomed to riding in a saddle and her position suffered because of that.

Cap had been helping and there was already improvement. By the end of the summer, Emma would have acquired an entirely new set of skills she was comfortable with.

I watched as Emma popped him over a small course and Cap came over to me.

"What's holding Emma back is her complete lack of interest in the finer points," Cap said. "Her instinct is to stay on."

"Whether it's pretty or not."

"It's never mattered before. She took riding at school to fulfill her physical education requirement. I don't think it made a big impression on her."

"No one is forcing her to do this."

"I think we should let Poppy ride him next week."

Cap paused. "I think it's Mill's influence. He's very competitive."

Emma pulled up at the top of the ring.

"That's good. You can take him into the woods if you'd like," Cap called to her.

Emma grinned and trotted out of the ring and up the driveway.

"Did Mill want her to play polo?" I asked as we walked toward the barn.

"Their father plays. That was the family sport. From what little was said, I gathered that Emma didn't think she could reach their level of expertise, so went in the opposite direction—bareback trail riding. What else could she do if she loved to ride?"

"Maybe she should be riding jumpers and not hunters."

"Maybe, but Emma still needs the basics."

"She could just exercise the horses while she's here," I said.

"But if she won a championship and could push the trophy in Mill's face, that would be a very satisfying moment for Emma. I know that even if she never said it."

"Is that how you felt about him?"

"I was a latecomer to the family. The dynamics are all different when you didn't grow up in the situation."

That sounded about right to me.

"I think we should let Poppy ride Available next week."

"She hasn't outgrown Tango," Cap replied.

"It'll be good for her even if her legs are a little too short."

***

Lockie was pulling on a change of clothes when I arrived at the carriage house.

"How do you feel?"

"I'm fine," he replied.

I looked at him.

"I slept off the headache."

"Why is it so hard for you to just say these things?"

"Because I don't want you to worry. I will always have headaches and they will always go away."

I kept looking at him.

"Ninety-nine percent of the time." He pulled the shirt over his head. "We don't know, Tal. We don't know about tomorrow for you either."

"I don't want to see you in pain."

He put his arms around me. "If that's true, where are my flowers?"

"I brought you a chocolate covered Oliver marshmallow."

Lockie kissed me. "For most of my life, I wouldn't consider spending time on a summer afternoon sitting anywhere but in a saddle. Would you sit in the raft with me for twenty minutes?"

"We'll paddle around the pond and Parti can chase us at the water's edge," I replied.

That colt loved to play at the pond.

"Soon a crowd will gather and ask what the heck we're doing," he said.

"What are we going to be doing?"

"Being together."

***

I spotted him on Lupino AF, one of our sales prospects Lockie was showing the coming weekend with Cam. The young gelding could jump, but what he did less well was listen. There were times when faced with a course, I was sure his mind went blank. A big horse, when he began galloping, the gas pedal got stuck. Lockie had tried to dial back the enthusiasm, or maybe it was anxiety, by quiet work.

We knew where he had come from and a lot had been expected of Pino. Lockie wasn't the kind of trainer who wanted to win at any cost. Fortunately, we weren't making performance demands and there was time to make adjustments in the gelding's favor.

19

Exercises to increase Lupino's flexibility and transitions to enhance his collection were designed to have the horse concentrate more on his frame than stretching out to achieve top speed. Two months ago, he couldn't stand still under saddle without fidgeting. Now he could.

"What do you think?" Lockie asked.

"Cam has a good eye for potential but..."

The gelding was a prospect Cam found out West and had shipped back early in the spring. Turnout had been the first order of business, then gradual work until Cam and Lockie decided he could go Pre-Green.

"What?"

"I don't think Pino's an upper level candidate. Not for a couple years, maybe not ever."

"Why?" Lockie rode over to me, halted, and dismounted.

"He needs to be bored. Until that happens, until he stops over-reacting, we can't tell what his capabilities are."

He flipped the stirrups over the saddle. "I think you're right. There are lots of jobs he can do successfully without ever jumping four foot."

We led Pino from the ring.

"He just needs to be put in the right situation."

"That's not hard. We found the perfect place for CB," Lockie replied.

Freddi came out of the barn. "Want me to take him for a walk?"

"Keep him out for about an hour," Lockie said, boosting her into the saddle. "Cross the stream, and don't avoid anything that could startle him."

"They're working a field down at the end of the road. That should be a treat."

We watched them walk up the drive to the open gate where they entered the field.

"Where are the *Zuckerwuerfel*?"

"Cap took the three girls out. They should be back soon."

"Let's do the pond and raft and floating thing."

"Okay."

We went to the shed, got the inflatable raft, and brought it to the pond. Parti saw us and trotted over. It was the first time he had seen the raft and he didn't know what to make of it. As we got on and pushed off from the bank, Parti raced back and forth, tail up, bucking, snorting, and tearing up the ground, soft after overnight rain.

"As if the farm is so quiet and nothing ever happens here," I said, watching the colt do a sliding stop and a rollback. "He's going to hurt himself."

"No, he's not."

Parti began pawing the water, splashing himself with a deluge, then he entered the pond and began coming toward us.

"So much for being alone," I said.

Lockie paddled us toward the other side and Parti followed.

"Go away!"

"He's not going to drown."

"Who taught him how to swim? His mother?"

The colt was gaining on us.

"What is he going to do with us when he gets here?"

"The worse that happens is we tip over and swim to shore."

I looked at Lockie in surprise. "Oh yes, I want to be in the water with flailing hooves." I waved the colt off, but that didn't deter him.

"What are you doing?" Poppy called from the bank.

I had no easy answer to shout across the water.

Lockie's phone began ringing, so he stopped paddling to answer it. I grabbed the paddle and began digging at the water to try to get to the shore before Parti attempted to sit next to me.

"That's not how you do it," he said.

"Me?" I asked.

"Yes. Will you please wait a minute?"

"Me?" I asked.

"No. Rhonda."

I slapped the paddle against the water to shoo Parti away. Maybe he thought it was a game and swam faster toward us.

"Who's Rhonda?"

"Hang on," he said.

"Me?" I asked.

Parti put his nose on my arm.

"No. Talia. Relax." Lockie handed me the phone. "Don't let it get wet." He took the paddle.

Gincy, Cap, and Annie had joined Poppy and they were all laughing at Parti's antics.

A moment later, we reached the bank and Cap leaned forward to help me get to the ground. Parti leaped out of the water, shook himself, and made it rain for everyone.

"Change of plans for the next two hours. We have someone coming to look at Windaway. Let's get him cleaned up and looking as sharp as..."

"One of Jules's knives," I supplied.

"A billionaire in a custom-made tuxedo," Cap added.

"A singer who got voted off a talent show," Lockie said.

"Good one," I replied.

"Hoof glitter?" Poppy asked, hopefully, as we walked to the barn.

"Hoof polish is sufficient, but you just concentrate on polishing up those ponies of yours and we'll have session," I said.

The three girls ran ahead of us.

"Cap, you take the girls and Tali will stay with me."

"Sure. What do you want them to do, Tal?"

"I was going to work on the basic dressage test. Make sure the transitions are at the letters, not a stride or two later."

"With stirrups?"

"Yes. Do the test three times, but switch ponies each time."

Cap laughed.

"Devilish." Lockie put his arm around my shoulders. "I like it."

An hour later, when Rhonda Stossel and her client arrived, Windaway was standing on the aisle, glistening from the tip of his ears, to the end of his banged tail. The gelding was a nice prospect who had some work but was still green. By next spring, he'd be ready to take on, if not the world, then regional shows in the pre-green hunter division.

After the introductions, I got on and rode to the indoor while Lockie told the two women about Windaway's background. Even though I rode every horse who came to the farm, I had only been on this one once. Cap had done most of the exercising and working with Lockie on the gelding.

He wasn't a complicated horse and I thought that quality would serve him well in life. Horses who had thoughts and requirements, like CB, wound up with impatient trainers who multiplied the severity of any issue.

We warmed up, did the simple exercises that would show the horse off in the best light and then brought him over for the client to ride.

"Was he ridden this morning?" she asked.

"No. He was outside all night and was on the schedule for late afternoon." I slid off. "We've been trail riding him. It's an easy way to condition a horse and less stressful than training every day."

"How long did you lunge him before we arrived?"

I gave her a leg up. "We were out on a raft in the pond playing with my sister's two year old when Rhonda called. All we did was shine him up for you, take the shavings out of his tail, and get my pony riders squared away."

She didn't trust us. I understood that. It wasn't personal. Maybe the last barn had misrepresented the horse she tried and being lied to bothered her. I didn't blame her for that.

We didn't need to pad a horse's resume. We weren't an equitation barn, or hunter or jumper. We had horses in training. Some were further along than others. Some had specific talents. We were fortunate not to have the pressure of money working against our horses. If we had a few bad months, the bank wasn't going to foreclose. My father would probably give us a long lecture about budgets, though.

I stood by while the woman settled into the saddle and then moved off, hoping she wasn't predisposed to disliking

Windaway because of her recent horse-hunting disappointments.

In sales situations with a trainer, Lockie was there to answer questions but he left the rest to the customer and coach. He always laid out everything important while the horse was being ridden by one of us.

If there was no coach, Lockie would take over, attempting to make it a positive experience for the horse and customer. Sometimes, Cap would take them for a short trail ride, making sure to cross the stream to prove there was no fear of water.

Lockie and I went to the entry of the indoor so Rhonda could have some privacy with her client, but never so far away that we could be accused of abandonment.

We could see the pony riders doing their dressage test—Gincy on Tango, Annie on Beau and Poppy on Spindrift. To our right, Dina was hand-grazing Twisty, just wanting to spend time with him.

"I think I'll go to Long River with Cam on Thursday so we can have all of Friday on the grounds," Lockie said.

It made sense. Otherwise, he would be rising very early Friday morning and facing a long drive, part of it in the dark. The headlights of oncoming traffic remained a problem for him even with the special contract lenses.

"That's a good idea."

"You'll be okay holding down the fort?"

"Sure. Friday will be normal. Saturday I have a pie judging contest."

"Excuse me?"

"Jules was asked to judge at the County Fair and requested moral support."

"I understand that."

"While I'm gone, Cap can help the Zucks get ready. Sunday we'll all go to the show at the fairgrounds."

"You're not thinking about Ami Gish, are you?"

"Greer gave me a stern talking to about holding your head high when insults are being cast in your direction."

Lockie turned back to check on Rhonda for a moment. "I never told you about one of the first jobs I had. I lasted for one show. He was in the observation area, drinking from mid-morning. This guy was the poster child for the excesses of new money. We had a rail down in the stakes class and he spent five minutes screaming at me so that everyone in the state could hear how incompetent I was. With people like that, it's not enough to end the relationship, they have to grind you into the dirt."

"What did you do?"

"Before he could say the magic words, with a crowd gathered around us, I quit saying there was no amount of money or prestige that would make me stay in that situation."

"I'm sorry."

"Don't be. Everyone there could see he was a mean drunk. Not many years later, he wound up in prison for embezzlement. Today, I'm a free man in white breeches and he's wearing an orange jumpsuit."

"How long did it take for you to get another position?"

"I was walking back to the trailer and Vita Shearer came up to me. She was looking for someone and I turned out to be that person. I spent two years on her estate in Northern Virginia, riding some of the finest horses in the country."

"Why did you leave?"

"Vita passed on and her family doesn't have the passion for horses that she did."

"I hope the farm wasn't turned into a housing development."

Lockie shook his head. "No, Jeffrey Berman owns it now. I rode for him, too, until I went to Germany."

That we were losing farms and open space at what I considered an alarming rate and few other people did, upset me even more. A dairy herd couldn't exist on the town park. Front lawns couldn't be hayed. Where were horses and riders supposed to gallop free?

Mr. Auerbach would eventually retire, and what would happen to his farm?

Bittersweet would stay in the family forever. I had made that vow years ago but I wondered about the fate of Rowe House Farm. Would Victoria lose interest and sell it or would she do the right thing and give it to Greer? At least if she gave it to Greer, I'd be able to reason with her about keeping it. I wasn't sure I could persuade Victoria to keep it. The farm was far more expensive to keep than Dice.

Lockie rubbed my back. "Want to go out to dinner tonight?"

"Really?"

"Maybe there's a square dance somewhere."

I bumped my shoulder into his.

Rhonda and her client walked out of the indoor.

"Would it be possible take him out on a trail, just to see his temperament?"

"Sure," I said. "Cap, are you done?"

"We can be," she called back.

"Have them accompany Windaway to the logging trail and then come home."

"Okay." Cap walked to the gate and opened it.

The large horse and the medium ponies walked up the driveway.

"He's nice," Rhonda said. "We've been looking for six months and this is the first horse she's serious about."

She had very high standards, I thought, but was smart enough not to say so aloud.

"As long as you're there to work with them, he'll turn into a very respectable ami-owner hunter," Lockie replied. "I like green horses to have a professional nearby."

"He'll be staying at my barn, and one of my working students will be doing most of the training sessions."

I knew how that was. People had jobs and lives. They didn't have the time to spend with their horses the way we did.

"Let's talk price," Rhonda said.

I got up from the picnic table. "I have work to do so I'll get to it. Nice to have met you, Rhonda, and I hope everything works out even if Windaway doesn't go home with you."

"Thank you."

I headed off to find Greer so we could create a schedule for the weekend.

3

AROUND MID-MORNING, just when the 4-H girls were finishing their last lesson before the fair, a trailer pulled into the yard.

"Talia! Who's that?" Poppy asked, always excited to see a trailer because there was the promise of a new horse— like a Christmas present under the tree.

"It's Twisty's ride home," I replied. "Would you go up to the house and ask Jules to fix a container of coffee and a snack for the driver?"

"Don't let anything exciting happen without me," she said and began to run to the house.

Poppy stopped at the back of the trailer.

Dina came out of the barn leading Twisty as the driver lowered the ramp and I heard hooves.

"Trade," she said.

An adorable dappled, dark brown large pony walked out of the trailer.

"What's his name?" Poppy asked, rushing to him.

"Knock Knock," Dina said.

"Who's there?" Poppy asked.

Dina laughed. "No, that's his name. Knock Knock."

"That's so cute!"

"Why don't you put him in Twisty's stall and Cap will help you make him comfortable."

"Yay."

Poppy and the pony walked to the lower barn.

"You didn't have to give me a pony."

"I collect them, too," Dina said. "You have all these riders, now you won't be missing a pony. Knock is honest and safe, you'll love him."

"Of course, I will. He's a pony."

***

Jules had prepared a picnic lunch for everyone and Lockie returned from Acadiana with Cam just in time to sit down for the grilled chicken sandwiches, carrot and beet salad and raspberry lemonade.

"Where's Gracie?" Cam asked, helping himself to some of everything.

"She went to an Ambassador of Good Cheer meeting," Jules replied, sitting next to me.

"I thought..." Cam started.

"What?" I asked when he didn't finish the sentence.

"There would have been time to take a ride but," he said looking at Lockie, "we might as well leave for Long River."

I was going to protest that there were riders and horses, but we weren't substitutes for Greer. The trail ride was just an excuse for the two of them to be in proximity.

"Cap, do you want to go with us?" Lockie asked.

"Is that okay?" Cap asked me.

"We're fine. We have lots of help here."

As long as we started afternoon chores around three, there was plenty of time to get everything done before dark. Greer wasn't expected back until dinner, having scheduled the appointment so that she would be sure to miss Cam's departure.

Lockie's phone began ringing.

"Lockie Malone," he said then listened. "It's for you." He handed the phone to Cam, who never carried a cell phone.

"What?" Cam said, then grimaced. "Okay. We'll be right there."

He handed Lockie the phone. "There's a problem with the truck."

Lockie stood. "Does it run?"

"No."

Acadiana had the newest and finest rigs, but there are many moving parts in an engine, and any one of them can fail at any time. This seemed to be one of those times. It was so much better to happen in the yard than on highway.

"You can take the van if you need it," I offered.

It was hardly a solution when there were more than three horses going and that's what the Bittersweet van held, but it was something in an emergency. That great and ancient van my father had gotten, thinking we'd lose interest in horses and there was no need to get anything fancy, had never stranded us on the road.

"I'll call you later when I know more." Lockie leaned over and kissed my cheek, then left.

"Buck up, girl," Jules said softly.

"What do you mean?"

"You get that expression every time he leaves."

I sighed.

"He'll be back. He doesn't have his clothes."

"Can you always find the positive in any situation?"

"That or chocolate."

***

With Lockie and my father gone, we decided to have a girls' night in. Greer stopped for Chinese food on her way home and I helped Jules make toffee-covered popcorn and cashews. We added the extra nuts into the Chinese food. I was in heaven.

The movie was one I never heard of but neither Greer nor I had spent much time watching television. Jules said it was one of those mismatched love stories. Take two people who couldn't possibly ever meet, shouldn't even like each other, and they fall in love. Hilarity ensues.

I thought it was a good excuse to sit between Jules and Greer. The movie was unimportant.

"Mrs. Meade told me about a horse—"

"Yes. Gincy was very upset about it."

"How do you not worm your horse?" Greer asked. "Must have been not ever."

"At least, it was saved."

The horse colicked due to the parasite load but fortunately, it ended fairly well. It would have been better if the horse had gone to a different home, but the world was not a perfect place.

"We have to do something."

"We've done stable management with the Zuckerlumpens. Do you think a video would be helpful?"

"That's a good idea," she said. "We could get the Waynes up here."

"We could do several short videos on the basics of horse care."

"Okay. I want to actually do something."

"Like handing out tubes of wormer on the street corner?"

"Yes! Exactly!"

"How?"

"At the 4-H Fair."

"Everyone there knows the importance of worming their horses."

Greer regarded me as if I was impossibly slow on the uptake. "The point is to raise awareness."

I thought for a moment. "Could we get a vet to sit in a tent for a couple hours and run McMaster tests on fecal samples? Then we could give out wormer." I paused. "How much is this going to set us back?"

"It won't be that much. Call it publicity."

Jules came into the den with a large bowl of popcorn. "What's publicity?"

"We want to raise awareness about the importance of worming your horse and were talking about offering information and wormer at the 4-H Fair."

"Good," Jules replied.

Greer took a handful of popcorn. "Can you invent a lollipop as a giveaway item for the human?"

"Not with the worm in it, I hope." Jules shuddered.

"Why did that even occur to you?" I asked.

"Tequila lollipops have worms in them," Greer explained.

"Don't tell me you ever ate something like that," I replied.

"No, I did not. But it was offered. Such things are beneath me. I have always maintained a baseline of standards. Might not have looked like it."

Jules reached over me and patted Greer's arm. "You know how to comport yourself like a lady."

Greer shrugged. "I didn't always manage it."

"That's in the past," Jules replied, holding out the bowl. "Have some more popcorn. This is where they meet cute."

***

A couple hours later, after the movie proved two incompatible people in love could conquer whatever Organized Crime, the high fashion world, and Broadway musical stars could throw at them, I got into bed, leaving Greer in the next room making plans for the Fair. All I had on my phone was a text message from Lockie assuring me that they had arrived at the show ground, and he was fine.

There was tap at my door just as I turned off the light.

"Come on in, Greer," I said.

The door opened. "How did you know it was me?"

"There are only three of us in the house, unless Dad came home quiet as a mouse, which is uncharacteristic for him."

Greer walked over to my window and looked out.

"What's wrong?"

"That movie. Do you think Jules had an ulterior motive for making us sit through it?"

"Excuse me?"

"Why?"

"She needed a reason? Okay. It was the one on tonight. It was a romantic comedy. No one died. No horses or small animals were harmed during the making of the movie. Nothing should have set either of us off, but apparently she was wrong."

"Did that Eleanora character remind you of me?"

My mind ground to a halt as I struggled to understand the question in Greer-speak.

"You're taking a long time to come up with an answer so you must have seen it, too."

"Seen what?"

"She was so brittle."

I had to replay this stupid movie I hadn't paid much attention to in order to see if there was any connection.

"I got nothing. Just tell me."

"She was so demanding! She was distant. Cold. Jules is sending me messages!"

"Wow. No. Jules is not sending you messages. If you believe that, you better put some tin foil around your helmet with a couple antennas and tuner knobs so you can pick up the right frequency."

"I'm like that."

"No."

"Cam didn't even say goodbye to me."

It always swings wildly back to him.

"You arranged it so you wouldn't be here to see him off. Cam wanted all of us, meaning you, to take a trail ride with him, but when he found out you wouldn't be home for hours, he decided they'd both leave for Long River after lunch."

Greer dropped onto the bottom of my bed. "He wanted to go on a trail ride?"

"Yes."

"That's how the blinking cow behaved."

The character in the movie.

Was it always so hard to keep up with Greer?

"You never went through this with Lockie, did you?"

"No—"

"Because you knew how he felt about you!"

"You've got it backwards. He felt something for me because he liked—I'm not saying this makes sense—how I behaved. Not the first few days, because I was horrible."

"I was worse."

"You were, I agree. He saw us at a show months before he met Dad. I was trying to help a pony rider, then Rui yelled at me."

"Rui yelled at you? You should have told me. We could have taken him behind the stabling and taught him a lesson."

"You weren't talking to me in those days."

Greer was quiet. "I was a bitch."

"Yes, but not now. Just act like the best possible you with Cam. You're kind and have ideas to do good that I wouldn't think of."

"That's not true."

"It is. I look for ways to help my students. You want to create organizations and programs in order to reach many people. That's your talent. It's a gift."

"If that's true, I got it from my grandmother. Grandmother Swope, never Rowe."

I couldn't help but laugh.

"I don't know. I've never been my best possible self."

"Then he's seen you at your worst and he's still interested."

Greer slid into the bed beside me. "That's the point. What if he likes evil Greer? What if he doesn't like the Greer you think I am?"

"He calls you Gracie."

"Exactly. Teasing me. Mocking me."

"Affectionately," I said.

"Are you sure?"

"Yes."

"May I stay with you tonight?"

I should have said no. An hour later she was still telling me about the worming booth at the 4-H Fair.

4

THE SKY was the color of dirty paper at midmorning and the yard seemed empty without Lockie, Cap and Cam. The weather forecast was for rain showers but not a downpour.

I was trying to do as much as I could, knowing I'd be away at the County Fair for most of the following day even though Jules assured me we'd be home in two shakes of a lamb's tail.

That's what I figured. That we'd be watching the lambs, tails and all, then the tractor pulls, quilting, and saying hi to Mr. Auerbach's team, Daisy and Rufus.

Greer was on the phone, organizing everyone's lives, coming out of her office periodically for updates. "The

Waynes are busy for the next two weeks. Is the week of the 4-H Fair good for you?"

I said yes to everything because it was easier than the truth. It was hard enough to schedule a morning without conflicts. Predicting what Wednesday two weeks away would be like was impossible.

The Zuckerlumpens were very excited to star in a new video. They would demonstrate how to put a tube of wormer medicine in their ponies' mouths. This would prove size and strength weren't required.

There was only one obstacle to complete success. We didn't have a vet who would sit at the 4-H Fair and run the McMaster test on the manure samples. Dr. Fortier was already scheduled to attend a show, and everyone else in the practice was needed at the office.

"This is only a small speed bump," Greer insisted, as she made a list of scenes for the video.

"Having a vet run the test is the center of gravity for the event."

"There are a hundred vets within a hundred miles, we'll find one."

"Can you take any of this confidence you display so easily and apply it to Cam?"

Greer glared at me. "Let's stay on topic, shall we? There is a great deal to accomplish and no need to talk about personal issues."

"You can't solve this by avoiding it."

43

"I have a plan."

Poor Cam. If he was part of her plan, he didn't stand a chance.

Her phone rang. "Greer Swope."

"I'll go," I said softly, beginning to move away.

She motioned for me to stay.

"Hi. Yes? That's wonderful. I'll have to thank him. Certainly. Come right over if you're in town. Stay for lunch if you'd like. See you in a few." Smiling, Greer put the phone down.

"Who was that?"

"I said it was a small speed bump. That was Dr. Denise Newbold, who just opened a practice nearby. Dr. Fortier called her, related our predicament and she's happy to help us."

"You have the Midas Touch or whatever it would be called. If I tried to do what you do in a morning, it would take me six weeks."

"The Grandma Swope Touch, trademark pending. She can get anyone to do anything. The vet's coming for lunch so tell Jules to be prepared for another person. We can have a nice talk with her and explain what we're trying to do."

I brought the pony riders up to the house with me and gave them the job of preparing the table under the trees, while I helped Jules place popsicles in waxed paper bags and then back in the freezer.

"No funny flavors, I hope."

"Fruit," Jules replied.

There were any number of exotic fruits that could only be enjoyed with an acquired taste so that was hardly a reassuring announcement.

"White cherry."

That sounded good. "What were the green ones? Wheat grass?"

She smiled. "Kiwi fruit and mint. I think I've lost your trust."

"I'm just a country girl."

"That's why we're going to the Farmhouse Restaurant tonight."

I groaned. "Is it like that pea pod place?"

"No, it's a real farm house and almost everything comes from the farm itself."

"Another girls' night out?"

"We have been abandoned. Have you heard from Lockie today?"

"Yes. Hours ago. He was very busy and someone asked him to ride a horse for them."

"You can do that?"

"I can't. He can. Very easily," I said. "I don't want him to do too much. It's August, hot and humid."

Jules put her hand on my arm. "Cap will keep an eye on him."

As I nodded, Poppy ran inside. "The vet's here."

"Okay. Go to the truck and introduce yourself then bring her here."

"I can do that!" Poppy ran outside.

"They are like coiled springs."

"All the time," I replied, as we went out to the terrace. "They never get tired."

Poppy was nearly skipping down the walkway leading the vet by the hand.

"Here she is!"

"Thank you for helping me, Poppy," Dr. Newbold said.

"Any time," she replied and danced off to play with Joly.

"You're not working them hard enough."

"Obviously. I'm Talia Margolin and this is Jules Finzi."

"Hi."

We all shook hands.

"I don't stand on ceremony," she said. "Just call me Denise. If you say Dr. Newbold, I'll think you're talking to my father."

"Is your father a vet, too?" Jules asked.

"Orthopedic surgeon. It was very helpful given how many times I fell off as a kid."

We walked to the picnic table and the girls had done a pretty good job bringing everything out.

"We heard about that horse," I said, not wanting to be more specific and be overheard by Gincy, "and my sister and I thought we could do something. We'd like to have a table at the 4-H Fair, run McMasters for anyone who brings a sample for testing, and give them an appropriate tube of wormer if their horse needs it."

"That's a great idea," Denise said. "I'm a one-person office so if I agree to sit there, I may be called away."

"That's fine. The animals always come first."

"Not to be too nosy, but what's the funding?"

"Jules had a terrific idea to make fake worm lollipops. People can buy them and that will cover some of the cost. We're not really worried. My sister is a genius at holding charity events."

"Finally, someone thinks I'm a genius," Greer said as she approached us. "I'm Greer Swope. We spoke on the phone."

"The answer is yes," Denise said. "We can talk about how we'll organize it, and hand out some pamphlets."

"Would you be able to give a brief demonstration of running the test?" I asked.

"Sure."

"Would you be comfortable if we did a video of that?" Greer asked.

Denise looked surprised.

"We've done a few instructional videos and posted them on viewtube. This would be good information to have on the Internet. Poppy and Gincy are going to demonstrate proper technique with a tube of wormer."

"If they don't get it all over themselves when the ponies try to spit it out," I commented.

"We'll put them in Hazmat suits," Denise said with a
wink.

***

Late in the afternoon, all chores done, all riders gone
home, I was changing into something nicer to wear to
dinner when my phone rang.

I hadn't heard from him all day but we had gotten a call
from Cap saying everything was fine and she was keeping
an eye out on him. The high temperature and humidity
concerned me, not only for Lockie, but the other riders and
most definitely the horses.

The heat made activity more of a physical stress. I
remembered one flat class Greer and I had ridden in late on
a summer day during which a girl fainted and fell off her
horse. There was no shade in an outdoor arena.

"Hi."

"Hi," Lockie said.

He sounded tired to me but I wasn't going to bring it up.

"Are you up at the house for dinner?"

"No, we're going out. The three girls. Jules found a place
she thinks will provide an interesting experience."

"So does an amusement park but the food stinks."

"This is farm house cooking on a wood stove. Yum."

48

"Just where everyone wants to be when it's 95 degrees out, standing over a wood-fired stove."

"Maybe they have air conditioning. Or a fan."

Lockie laughed. "I won't keep you from your ladies night out. I won two of the hunter classes."

"Well done!"

"We're going out for dinner, too—business, and probably won't be back to the room before you turn in, so I wanted to let you know we're all fine. Do you believe me?"

"Of course."

***

The restaurant was a farmhouse.

"Rustic," Greer commented as we drove up and parked alongside several cars from the city.

It was a beautiful location with views of the hills and green fields. The cow barn was far enough away so the odor wasn't apparent to me but I was smelling manure all day long so all of that was normal.

Following the wooden arrows to the front door, we entered and were shown to a table in what was at one time the sitting room. Single sheets of paper were handed to us as the menus.

"It's so hard to make a decision from all these choices," Greer commented.

There was a vegetarian option or a carnivore option. I was stuck.

Jules flagged a waitress down. "Can you be a little more specific about what protein is being served?"

"It's chicken today," the pretty young girl replied. "It's very good. Buttermilk fried chicken. If you choose it, let me warn you that there will be a wait. Some people go outside and take a walk through the garden."

Greer handed her the menu. "Chicken."

Jules and I agreed.

"Would you like your salad now or with the meal?"

"Now, and then we can go outside?" I asked.

"That sounds lovely," Jules said, not looking at Greer.

I wanted Greer to get into the spirit of the adventure but she had wilted in the heat of the day and Cam hadn't called her. He never called, I could understand why not, but Greer thought Cam should have psychic abilities and know she wanted him to call.

She could, of course, call him—either through Lockie or through the motel, but then someone would know.

It had taken me quite a bit of contemplation to understand the dynamic, but now that I did, it made sense. Greer Sense.

Our salads arrived and were put in front of each of us.

"Oh no," Greer said softly.

I picked up a fork.

"Make sure that's clean," she told me.

"What's wrong?" I asked, because it was required.

"The salad is in a little tin pie plate."

"Cute," Jules replied.

"None of the silverware matches. None of the glasses match."

"Do you want to go home," I asked, "or go to the Grill Girl and come back for us in two hours?"

"You don't want me here."

"No, I want you to be happy. I don't want you to get to dessert and have been miserable the entire time."

"It's just a meal, Greer," Jules said. "If you're still hungry when we get home, I'll fix you something."

I ate a forkful of salad. "It's good. The greens are fresh out of the garden. It's like a still life oil painting." I speared a tomato and held it up. "Look at these beautiful purple cherry tomatoes."

"With dirt on them?"

Jules and I had to laugh.

In the other room, there came a great bellowing. At first, I thought a cow had gotten inside but quickly realized it was a city person complaining. About everything. The wait, the lack of fine china, calico napkins, the soft ground outside, and his companion's heels had sunk in. Those shoes that cost a fortune now were covered in manure.

"Parvenu," Greer said, picking up a fork. "One does not discuss the price in public."

"Good rule," I replied and continued eating.

"I need to apologize."

Jules smiled encouragingly at her. "You may do so any time."

"Isn't that offer sufficient?" Greer asked. "Having the thought and intention?"

I knew my sister well enough to know she was teasing us, but her performance was so flawless no one else would suspect. No one but Cam.

After finishing our salads we had a wait for the chicken, so we took a walk around the garden then came back inside just in time to see Mr. Bullmoose City Man flip his credit card at the hostess to pay for the meal.

Lady Greer walked up to him. "Have a nice night and be sure to tell all your friends what a lovely time you had in the country."

Her regal demeanor made it impossible for him to snap back at her so he huffed, took his companion's arm, and nearly pushed her outside.

"Very nice," Jules commented as she walked around the room to see the old family photos hung on the walls.

"Maybe we'll get lucky and he'll convince his friends this is a right little hellhole, and they'll buy weekend houses in the Hamptons instead," Greer said to me.

"They're so snooty. If I go to town in my barn clothes, they're looking down on me."

"If I catch one of them doing that to me—"

Greer was not the kind of person who figured out the perfect thing to say twenty minutes too late. Besides, when she channeled the Rowe side of the family, her presence made most people behave.

"I hope I'm there."

Jules motioned us to the table where our chicken had just been served on larger vintage pie pans. The food was delicious and we all agreed that should my father, Lockie and Cam ever be home at the same time, we would return for another farmhouse dinner.

5

GETTING ON CB early the next morning, we worked for about fifteen minutes, and then ponied Parti for a short walk through the fields. The heat and humidity were predicted to be similar to the day before, so everyone wanted to do as much as they could by late morning.

While none of us saw the point in riding in the middle of the day, Lockie, Cam and Cap had no choice in the matter. Up to a point. We had agreed last year that no one would show in potentially dangerous conditions. Eight jumps in pre-green hunter was stress of a far lower magnitude than an open jumper course. Cross country, which we did not have to consider, would definitely not be approved by me under these conditions.

Knowing Lockie would assess that a fit athlete could tolerate more than an unfit one, we had agreed upon checking with a weather site's data-based calculations of the conditions—temperature, humidity, wind speed, sun. Science would decide. That and Dr. Fortier's suggestion of what conditions should be avoided.

Cap called midmorning to give me a status report and assured me all was well. She also said it was getting quite warm and humid. They had electrolytes on hand and the facility had a number of wash areas set up where horses could be hosed.

Leaving Greer with the pony riders and Day, I went to the carriage house to clean up. As I took my shower, my phone charging, I tried to put everything but pie out of my mind. It was one concern replacing another. Would these pies be iconic country pies or would there be creative expressions of the bakers' artistry like we saw on the cooking shows? Would the pie-makers cry if they didn't win? I didn't want to see anyone sobbing in disappointment by the milking machine demonstration.

Ten minutes later, Jules and I were on our way to the county fairgrounds. Halfway there I realized I left my phone on the charger.

"Do you have any idea how long this will take?"

"Talia, relax. Enjoy yourself."

"I left my phone at home."

"Two or three hours. He's busy. He'll call you later."

"What if he calls at lunch? What if—"

"If frogs had wings, they wouldn't drag their butts on the ground," Jules replied.

I thought about it for a moment. "What does that have to do with this?"

"I don't know. It's something my father used to say. Different wording though," Jules said as she turned the car into the fairground. "You have to make peace with temporarily not having the answers. Cap's at the show. If there's an emergency, I repeat if, she will call Greer. Greer will call me if your phone goes to voice mail. You will not know for two minutes instead of one."

I nodded. "A little over the top, huh?"

"You can be vigilant. We all understand and appreciate that concern." Jules parked the car and turned to me. "Be here now, be somewhere else later."

"Good advice."

"I need your help with the pies."

We got out of the car and found our way to the correct tent and the baked goods section.

"We're looking for a woman with a Marie Espe name tag," Jules told me as we walked through the tent.

There were quilt displays, jams, platters of cookies, a multitude of cupcakes and, of course, we passed the pies. A moment later, a pleasingly round woman appeared, hurrying toward us.

"Julietta?" she asked.

"Jules."

"Thank you so much for helping us out in a pinch. I don't know what we would have done without an expert to judge. Our contestants expect someone who is very knowledgeable about baked goods. It's not a matter of the pies tasting good, they must be correct."

Jules nodded. "I understand your dilemma. So many people would just like a piece of pie and a cup of coffee and be satisfied."

"That's it exactly. We want you to judge the quality of the crust. We need someone who can taste the difference between butter, lard or shortening."

"Crucial," I agreed. "If the bottom crust is soggy—"

"Catastrophe," Jules finished for me.

"I'm so relieved." Marie showed us to the table lined with pies and a chair. "Oh dear. I didn't realize you had an assistant. I'll find you another chair." She hurried off.

I studied the pies, some of which were quite sad looking.

"*Buongiorno.* Do you need a chair?"

A very handsome man with dark hair was holding a folding chair out to us.

"*Sì. Grazie,*" Jules replied.

"I speak English," he said with a smile that lit up the tent. "Diego Morosoli. And you fantastically lovely women are...?"

Smiling, Jules held out her hand. "Julietta Finzi."

Diego raised her hand to his lips and kissed it.

I didn't know men still did that. It was cute, but I wasn't going to offer my hand for similar treatment. "Talia Margolin."

"Mar..."

"Mar go lin," I repeated slowly.

"Si, yes. Margolin." He said as though he had always known. "Why are you here? Entering a cuppacake?"

"No cupcakes. We're judging the pies."

"*Torta*. Very good, these American desserts. Not like in Italy."

"No," Jules agreed.

"Italian desserts only in my restaurant," Diego said.

"You have a restaurant?"

He laughed. "What do you say? Watch this space. It will open next month."

"What's it called?" Jules asked.

"*Basta*."

I shook my head.

"Enough," Jules translated for me.

"I'm here," he pointed to the exit in the tent, "outside. I...rent, rented, a food truck for this."

I hoped Diego had a driver's license and knew what all the traffic signs meant.

"Publicity," he said. "I'll bring you...lunch. Spaghetti and meatball sandwiches."

Jules nodded and smiled while I wondered how the heck it was possible to turn spaghetti and meatballs into something you could hold like a sandwich.

"Ciao," Diego said and left the tent.

"He must have the words wrong," I said. "He can't mean sandwich."

"No, he can't."

"Cute."

"Oh, yes. Full of personality." Jules sat down and drew the first pie to her.

I handed her the knife.

"Here goes nothing."

"Bombs away."

She cut into the blueberry pie. "Now or never."

"Jetzt oder nie," I said.

"What does that mean?"

"Now or never. That's the name of Cam's horse."

"I didn't know that."

We looked down in dismay at the blueberry juices flooding the plate.

"I think she forgot to add a thickening agent."

"Cornstarch?" I asked.

Jules carefully lifted a piece of pie onto the plate between us. "Yes. Good memory. We'll have to start cooking lessons again."

I nodded but had no idea when there would be enough time.

I took a forkful of pie. "Forgot the sugar, too." It was like eating a lemon.

Jules made some notations on the sheet left for her, then looked around for a bottle of water but that was something the Fair Committee had forgotten. I had come prepared and pulled two bottles of water from my saddle bag and placed them on the table.

"You're a lifesaver."

"Me and the Boy Scouts. Ever vigilant."

"I think they're always prepared."

"Who's vigilant?" I asked, confused.

Jules cut into another pie. "It's not Betty Crocker so I don't know."

I laughed and we started the process over again.

About an hour later, we had eaten one bite each of it seemed like a hundred pies, in wildly divergent degrees of edible. The winner was obvious. The runners-up required discussion but not retasting as we both felt the next time we wanted pie would be Thanksgiving.

Maria came over to the table. "I wonder if we could ask a favor."

"What would that be?" Jules asked, trying not to commit to anything.

"Some of the contestants would like your expert opinion. Even if they didn't win, they'd like some feedback so they can do better next year."

Jules and I shared a look.

"It's sometimes done at horse shows," I said. "Not always."

I knew Jules didn't want to find twenty-five ways to avoid saying the pie was lousy.

"A few," Jules told Marie. "Not everyone."

Marie smiled. "They'll be very happy. May I have the list of the winners, so we can present the prizes and then I'll send the bakers to you."

"The winner is Mrs. Rachel Miller and her Bourbon Peach Pie. It was excellent. The crust was perfectly flaky and adding the pecans gave the filling just the right amount of texture." Jules gave her the list and off she went.

"This could be bad," I said.

"Very."

Diego came into the tent carrying a bag. "Lovely ladies, your lunch."

He began by placing napkins in front of us. The cans of Italian lemon soda were already starting to sweat and why not, so were we. Then, making a sweeping gesture, he placed the sandwiches on the table.

I studied mine in amazement.

"Pick up." Diego demonstrated taking a huge bite.

Instead of a roll, the spaghetti was compressed and fried so it would hold together. Between the two layers of spaghetti were sliced meatballs and melted mozzarella.

"*Mangia*," he said.

I took a bite. "*Delizioso.*"

"*Buono*," Jules agreed.

Diego's eyes sparkled in delight. "I'll watch you eat," he said, sitting on a chair he dragged from another table.

"Go back to your food truck," I said. "We know how to eat. No hints are required."

"Hints?" he asked.

"Instructions," I replied.

"Si."

He didn't leave, but the sad non-winners began arriving.

The first loser held out her pie to us. "I tried so hard," she said.

I remembered that pie. For the rest of my life I would remember that pie.

"On the label, it said coconut cream pie."

"Yes."

"I'm a little bit confused about the coconut in the pie. It didn't seem like any coconut I'm familiar with. What kind of coconut was it?"

"Celery."

Diego started laughing.

"Excuse me?" Jules said.

The woman glared at Diego. "Coconut is high in saturated fat so I don't use it because of the health concerns. Instead, I cut celery into thin slices and boil it until all the flavor has gone. Then I soak the celery in coconut flavoring."

Diego was laughing so hard, tears were coming to his eyes.

"Why don't you make chocolate cream pie?" I asked.

"No one in my family likes chocolate. They want coconut," the woman explained.

"In a competition," Jules said gently, "if you call a pie coconut cream, it needs to have actual coconut in it."

"I didn't think you'd be so particular," the woman said, and holding the pie close, walked away.

The next woman stepped up with her apple pie that I recognized all too well.

"What was wrong with my pie?" she asked defiantly.

"Did you taste it?" Jules asked in return.

"No. It's the same recipe I've used for years. The crust was good, wasn't it?"

"Yes, the crust was quite good, but the filling was very tart. What kind of apples did you use?"

"Green apples."

"Granny Smith?"

"No, the green apples on the tree outside."

I swallowed hard. "Unripe apples?"

The woman shrugged. "Yes. They're not poisonous. It's like green tomatoes. You can still use them."

Jules nodded. "Yes, but you need to compensate with more sugar."

She looked at us. "Oh."

Diego hadn't stopped laughing from the last contestant.

"He's not quite in the spirit of this exercise, is he?" I whispered to Jules.

"No."

"You Americans are so funny but I have to make more sandwiches. Maybe out of hoe cakes, whatever they are. Ciao, ladies."

The next person in line stopped in front of us with a scowl on her face. "I won three years in a row. Why didn't I win today?"

It went like that for the next half hour. Store-bought pie crusts, canned dinner rolls pressed flat, chai tea goop as filling. There were also beautiful pies made of sliced green tomatoes, berry pies and custards of surprising flavors. I thought the strawberry lemonade curd pie was very inventive, even if a strange color.

Finally, we were free to leave and rushed off the grounds before someone pushed more food at us.

"What would you like for dinner?" Jules asked on the way home.

"I don't know how you can think about eating. Between the pies and the fried spaghetti and meatball sandwich, I won't be able to look at food for a week."

"Morning buns for breakfast?"

"Yes, please."

6

WHEN WE GOT BACK to the farm, I found that the pony riders had gone to Peck's Pond for a swim. It was too hot to do anything else.

Greer and I sat together as she brought me up to date on the plans for the worming clinic and showed me the scene list for the video.

***

We put away all Greer's papers to start the afternoon chores when my phone rang. I could see it wasn't Lockie as I clicked it on.

"Everything is okay," Cap said.

"What happened?"

"Are you alone?"

"Greer's with me."

"Good. Lockie's in jail."

"What?" I shouted.

Greer looked at me in surprise and Joly ran into the hallway.

"There was a little altercation with a guy I don't know. Some shoving. I don't think there was a fist fight."

"Fist fight?"

Greer nearly stood on my foot in order to press her ear to the phone.

"Men do these things. And the man pressed charges."

"Does he need a lawyer? Should I drive out there?"

I tried to calculate how long it would take to get to the other side of the state.

"Cam's at the police station with him. He'll bail Lockie out, or whatever it takes, and then someone will call you. I have to go take care of the horses," Cap said. "I'll call you if I hear anything."

"Wait."

"There's nothing you can do," Cap assured me.

"There's always something you can do," I replied.

"No. Bye."

Cap was gone so I clicked the phone off.

"Lockie got in a fight and is in jail?" Greer asked.

"That's the gist of it."

"Don't freak out."

"I knew something was wrong."

"No, you didn't."

"I did! I told Jules on the way to the fair."

"You're always saying that. This time you happened to be right. It's a coincidence. The law of averages."

Jules entered the room. "What's all the shouting?"

"Nothing. Lockie's in jail is all."

"Why?"

"He got into a fight. I don't think Cap knows. Cam went to the police station with him. Should I drive to Long River?" I asked.

"No," Jules said. "You stay here. Calm down and we'll all wait to hear something."

"Someone must have provoked him," Greer said.

Or it was the heat, and a headache, and irritability.

"Cap knows him. How did it get this far?"

"Don't blame Cap. She was riding Spare. You can't send him out with a babysitter."

"He's a grown man, Talia," Jules said. "No matter what happened."

"You don't understand!"

"We do," Greer said. "Even if you did everything right. Even if you had a monitor on him and you were standing next to him all day long, the world is not under your control."

"You're making yourself crazy." Jules put her arms around me.

"I can't care less."

"No one's asking you to do that. We love you for that quality."

"Just dial it back a little," Greer said as she picked up Joly to reassure him.

"Greer," Jules said. "Not helpful."

"That's the bottom line."

Jules gave me a squeeze. "I know it'll be difficult but just in small increments get yourself to realize not everything is an emergency."

"Cam will take care of springing him from the slammer," Greer said.

"It sounds so much better when you put it in those terms," I retorted.

"Whatever it is, it will be handled," Greer replied and left the kitchen.

Jules nodded. "It will be."

"I'm going to go spend some time with CB."

"Good idea. Then you can help me with dinner."

CB and I walked to the end of the road, then turned onto the old logging trail. It felt like the rides I had taken with Butch to get away from everything. I had been unable to change my life then and I was unable to change anything that day.

Six students were counting on me to coach them at the County Fair Horse Show the following day and I couldn't imagine anything I wanted to do less. The ponies were in their stalls, braided and wearing sheets to keep them as clean as possible. The tack was freshly soaped. The saddle pads were washed and dried.

I wondered if I was making a mistake with the assignments for the show.

I wondered if I knew how to make the right decision about anything.

"How long could we live off the trail, Cee?" I asked him. "You'd be fine. I can't eat grass and leaves."

I had asked Butch the same kind of question many times, planning how it could be possible to run, or trot, away from home. A kid alone could disappear. A kid and a horse would be impossible to hide.

Would Butch be able to find his way back to the farm if I had gotten off and let him go?

That's the way it always played out in movies, the horse returned home without the rider and a lot of shouting was the result. I didn't believe that, though. I suspected Butch would just find the juiciest grass and stay there until someone came looking for him.

There were so many tactical drawbacks to running away that I never came close to having a plan, but it had always been enough to take my mind off my problems.

Now they weren't my problems, they were our problems. If I thought my reputation would be harmed by Paul Gish's lawsuit, Lockie being arrested for assault would not help his reputation, either. He knew better than to engage in a shoving match or worse.

Since he knew better, there had to be a reason.

I hoped it was a good one.

By the time I got back to the house, Greer had helped with dinner and Freddi had put out the horses for the evening. There was nothing left for me to do but try to eat dinner as we waited for Cam and Lockie to drive back from Long River.

Greer and I were sitting by the pond watching Joly playing among the cattails when the dark red Acadiana Farm car arrived.

As we were walking up to the terrace, Greer put her hand on my arm. "Don't overreact."

Right. "I'm not planning on it."

"Hi," Cam said with something of a smile.

"Hi," Greer replied.

"Are you okay?" I asked Lockie. "Do you need dinner?"

"I just want to go home and take a shower."

"Okay."

"Alone," Lockie said.

7

I NODDED. "Okay. Maybe I'll see you in the morning. I have the County Fair Horse Show with the girls, so we'll be getting an early start."

Lockie turned and headed toward the carriage house.

"Did the offer of dinner extend to me?" Cam asked.

"Of course."

We went to the kitchen door.

"Don't hold it against him. He didn't really talk to me either. Fun ride home."

"Cam would like some dinner," Greer told Jules.

"And Lockie?"

"Is going to spend the night at the carriage house," I replied.

Jules began removing bowls and containers from the refrigerator.

"So what happened?" Greer put Joly on the floor.

"He didn't tell me." Cam washed his hands at the sink then sat in his normal place at the table. "The police told me there had been a heated disagreement between Lockie and a Nadim Anter."

"Do you know who that is?" I asked.

"No."

"I never heard of him. So then what."

"Anter claims Lockie assaulted him but there were no witnesses to that, just that he fell to the ground."

"Were there any bruises or marks?" Greer asked.

"Haven't we been watching too much *CSI*," Cam replied. "I was able to bail Lockie out. The police didn't share the details of the case with me."

There was a case.

My stomach clenched at the word.

"Is this alleged victim a trainer, owner, rider or what?" Greer asked.

"Owner. Very wealthy, slimy owner." Cam began to eat.

"Did Lockie know him or was this just a case of instant dislike?" Jules asked, sitting across from Cam.

"I don't know that."

"If he is an owner, did he have horses at the show? Riders, grooms, crew?" Greer asked.

"I didn't see it happen. I saw him for a split second as he filed the charge against Lockie. We didn't go back to the show after Lockie was released on his own recognizance. I'm sorry I didn't turn into Columbo and begin questioning everyone on the grounds."

"Who's Columbo?" Greer asked.

"A famous television detective," Jules answered.

"Like Hercule Poirot? He was on the BBC. Like Hamish MacBeth? Like Miss Marple?"

In resignation, Cam shook his head.

"Are you going back to Long River tonight?" I asked.

"I'll go home and get a couple hours sleep and drive out early in the morning. I have my horses to ride and his, too."

"I'm sorry," I said.

"It's not a problem. Let Lockie do things in his own time." Cam finished dinner and got up to leave.

"Thank you for helping him."

Cam kissed my cheek, gave a wave and headed home.

"Don't be upset," Jules told me.

"Easier said than done, but I'll manage."

"I can make some of your favorite popcorn and we can watch a movie."

"Thanks, Jules, but I'll just get into bed and call the day done."

"Sure. I'll see you in the morning."

Jules kissed my cheek and I went upstairs to my bedroom.

When Lockie first came to the farm, I would look out my window and see his light on in the apartment over the barn. It made me feel connected to him. Cap wasn't on the farm, and I couldn't see the carriage house from my room. So I felt disconnected.

Getting into bed, I didn't pick up a book. Instead, I just turned out the light and rolled over. Between doing all the extra work at the farm, tasting all those pies and having the day end in something akin to chaos, I was exhausted and fell asleep immediately.

My phone woke me. I found it and clicked it on. "Hi."

"Is it too late to change my mind?"

"No." I pushed back the sheet and got up.

Lockie was walking down the drive as I was walking up to the carriage house. He put his arms around me.

"I'm sorry."

"It's okay. You had a big day and needed some time alone to accept being a jailbird."

He squeezed my hand. "I was held, that's all."

We started back up the drive, in silence for most of the way.

"Were you fingerprinted?"

"Yes, but my fingerprints are already on file."

"Why?"

"Gun permit."

"Why did you need one?" I asked.

"Whippers-in carry guns. Sometimes things happen on the hunt field that need to be stopped."

"Right."

He opened the door for me and I went inside.

"I woke you up. I'll let you get back to sleep."

We went up the stairs and I pulled off my sweats then got into bed. I felt half asleep as the pillow accepted my head.

"Talia?"

"Yes?"

"Don't you want to ask me what happened?"

"I want you to tell me whatever you need to say."

"Not knowing is as good as knowing?"

"Is it something you can make sure I will never find out?"

"Probably. There's what happened and there's the reason it happened."

"I would tell you," I said.

"You would. Would you cry in the shower before you did?"

"Maybe. I would cry if I was afraid it would change your opinion of me. Is that what your reluctance is?"

"I didn't do anything, but I was accused. I trained at Nadim Anter's ranch in California. There the main house, very grand, and the ranch houses, or outbuildings, for the ranch manager and some workers. He's very wealthy and a martinet. Fortunately, he wasn't on the property very often."

"This sounds like one of those stories that cannot have a happy ending."

"We're here together so that's a happy ending," Lockie replied. "Nadim had a couple jumpers and he had a daughter I was supposed to train. So I trained her when she showed up for our sessions, but mostly she was anywhere but the ranch. She knew how to be difficult. Not that I blame her."

"No wonder you didn't bat an eye when you got here."

"There is no comparison between either of you and Parisa. Aside from the fact that your father is not a mental case."

"My father is a decent man," I said.

"Very." Lockie paused. "Nadim was away on business for a few weeks. Nothing out of the ordinary happened until he came home. Something set him off, someone said something to him, intimating that Parisa and I had a relationship beyond the show ring. She came to my door at about eleven at night, crying, telling me he dragged her down the stairs by the hair."

"Geez."

"What was I supposed to do? I told her to call the police."

"Which is probably a stupid suggestion, given that you're making an accusation against a rich man."

"Exactly. She was too afraid of him to do that, so I told her to take the farm truck and go to a friend's house until this all blew over."

"That makes some sense," I admitted.

"She was just about to leave when Nadim came to the door. Just what he needed. Proof. Swearing in two languages, he slugged me. Fortunately, his power is in making money, not in fighting, and I saw it coming so all I had was a slight bruise."

"Did you go to a doctor?"

"No, I didn't. I put ice on it."

I was about to speak.

"It was less serious than getting in the way of a horse swinging his head around. Don't make more of it than that."

I felt like crying even if it happened before the accident.

"Nadim sent her off to live with relatives. I was fired and he made sure everyone in the community knew why."

"No one could believe it," I replied.

"Some people did. Life was a little difficult and then the opportunity to leave the country came up, so I left. End of story until we saw each other today and he started where we left off as if no time had passed at all. Push and shove. He fell. That was the perfect excuse to call the police and press charges."

This was awful almost beyond words. "Someone must have seen this happen, a witness to confirm your version of the incident."

"He must have seen me earlier on the grounds and followed me, waiting until no one was around."

"When billionaires attack," I commented. "Could be a good reality television program."

"He'd find a way to make money off of it." Lockie was silent for a moment. "That's the whole story."

It was unfortunate that he hadn't been able to take pictures of the incident on his phone the way Greer had done when she saw a top rider abusing her horse in Florida.

"I'm sorry."

"There's nothing for you to be sorry about."

"I want you to have a perfect life," I replied.

Lockie laughed and held me close. "I have a perfect life."

"Are you going back to Long River to finish your rides?"

"Nope. Cam is going to ride for me. I'll go with you, if you and the pony riders will have me."

"Of course. They adore you. To them, you're like a pop singer, like Truly Lambert."

"Who's that?"

"He's in a band called Maisie and The Boys' Night Out."

"Are they any good, or do they just wear tight pants?"

I laughed. "Very good and I don't know how tight his pants are since he's usually playing the piano."

"Loud?"

"No. You wouldn't be uncomfortable."

"Go to sleep, Tal. Tomorrow you will have to rebraid at least three tails."

We kissed goodnight and fell asleep.

8

POPPY WAS ABOUT TO MOUNT Tango for the pony hunter under saddle class.

"Hang on," I said. "How about you ride Beau and Gincy, you ride Tango?"

They looked at me in confusion.

Lockie was starting to smile, so turned away.

"I haven't ridden Beau," Poppy said.

"I only rode Tango once," Gincy informed me.

"I know. That's the point. We're here for experience."

They hesitated.

"Sounds like a good idea to me," Lockie said. "Come on, Gincy, I'll help you."

"Really? Gee." She blushed pink.

"But I'm entered on Tango," Poppy pointed out.

"I'll take care of it," I replied.

We got them on, sorted out, and began walking to the warm-up area.

"You planned this," Lockie said.

"Sure did. Entered Poppy on Beau and Gincy on Tango last week."

"Diabolical. I like it."

"They wanted to ride at the Fair because everyone they know is here, but aren't they really beyond it?"

"One could make that argument," Lockie replied.

"So I threw them a curve ball."

"Which one will have the more difficulty?"

I watched the girls trot around the field. "Poppy's a stronger rider and Tango is a little slicker but Beau is very reliable. Gincy is good on the flat. I don't know how it'll work out."

"It's a good way to learn where their weaknesses are," Lockie said. "Are they cubbing at the end of the month?"

"They want to. Poppy doesn't want to ride with the Hilltoppers anymore."

"I don't object, depending on the country, but I wouldn't want to see Tango trying to climb over some of the fences out there."

"I know. Maybe Keynote could pack her around."

I grimaced as Gincy was nearly run over by a small girl on too large a horse.

"Best thing to be riding in a warm-up area is a horse that's at least seventeen hands," Lockie commented as the little girl rode off toward the trees with her mother running after her.

Gincy pulled up at the farthest point of the area and seemed to be talking to a girl riding western.

"What's going on?" I asked.

Lockie turned to look. "You said they know a lot of kids here."

I shook my head.

A moment later, Gincy turned Tango away and trotted over to us.

"What's wrong?" I asked.

She was clearly upset. "Her name is Patty. She thinks she's all future zap."

Lockie looked at me.

"Translate," I said to her.

"Better than everyone."

"Good for her!" Lockie smiled. "In that case, we'll have to make it a point to watch a couple of her classes and pick up some tips."

"She said...mean things about you, Talia."

I put my hand on Gincy's knee. "It's not the truth, is it?"

"No." She was on the verge of tears.

"Ignore her. She upset you, and that's what she wanted. Some people don't know how to be nice. Feel sorry for her," I said.

"Doubly sorry. She's not going to get any marshmallow ice cream when she gets back to the barn like we will," Lockie added.

Gincy brightened. "Is that what we're having?"

"Could be," Lockie replied. "It's time to get to the in-gate, so go."

Gincy nodded then walked Tango away.

"I think we should rename the farm," I said as we followed her. "To Outlaw Farm."

"Where the training is so bad, it's criminal," Lockie replied.

"At least we're renegades together," I said.

His phone started ringing and he removed it from his pocket to look. "Cam. I have to get it. I'll find you by the rail."

I kept walking and stopped next to Aly Beck.

"At least it's not raining," she said.

"Today I'd welcome rain. It's eighty degrees and not even ten o'clock."

The pony hunters entered the ring.

"It's summer," Aly explained. "It's supposed to get hot."

Which reminded me, it was time to force a bottle of water on Lockie.

The class was asked to trot. Most ponies and riders complied quickly, others had to think about it for a little while. Some were doing a working trot, others were someplace between walking and jogging.

All of Gincy's dressage work was paying off as she was exhibiting nice control and using some inside leg on the corners. Poppy was her bold self, and found a spot on the inside track to show Beau off well. He was a little sleepy given the heat of the day, and I wasn't concerned about her waking him up. Sleepy was probably what the judge was looking for.

The ringmaster asked them to walk and then canter. That was the signal for the stampede, with some ponies worried they would be left behind and had to catch up, and some riders unable to understand the instructions.

Lockie came up alongside me. "How are they doing?"

"I hope they enjoy themselves because this is the last County Fair they're going to."

I wanted the Zuckerlumpens to compete against riders who were as serious as they were, and hopefully even more competent. They shouldn't be in an arena with ponies inventing their own class specs.

"There's a show at Balanced Rock in September. Take them to that."

The best ponies on the East Coast would be there. I didn't know that Gincy and Poppy had a chance to place but it certainly would be experience. The entry fees would also be substantial. Was that fair to the Becks and Hambletts? I wasn't sure.

"I'll think about it. What did Cam say?"

"He won the championship with Not That Far. And got him sold."

"Really? That's fantastic."

"Someone liked him very much and thought he was ready for the fall season."

The ponies had reversed and had just picked up a trot.

"I'm not needed," Lockie said, leaning against the rail.

"Not at all. Superfluous," I replied, teasing him in return. "Of course, you did win two classes with him and you're the one who trained the horse, so that counts for next to nothing."

"Cam could train."

"In his spare time away from Acadiana."

Determined to be a dressage rider, Gincy was making the mistake of riding Tango on the bit. Poppy had given up with Beau, and let his neck stretch out so far I hoped he wouldn't trip over himself.

"What happens if Poppy gets pinned on Gincy's pony?" Lockie asked into my ear.

"She adores you. You put a positive spin on it."

The ponies began cantering in the opposite direction.

"Can you bear to part with her a couple times a week?"

"Sure, but maybe it's better if you take both of them until school starts."

"Okay."

"Gincy's young and there isn't much she can do but train for a while but there are many riders in her same situation.

They're waiting to grow up a little. Next year we'll see how she's doing."

"And Poppy?"

"Pony jumpers. Pony vaulters. Pony ropers. She wants to do it all."

That was true. Poppy loved to ride, and go fast.

The ringmaster asked for the riders to line up, and they did, slowly and unevenly.

Both girls were out of the ribbons.

"This is why I don't like showing," I said to Lockie as we went to the out-gate. "Clearly, they should have gotten something."

"I agree."

"I have no idea what to say to them."

"Tell the truth. It's one person's opinion."

It was going to be a long day.

***

After dark, Cam and our horses returned to the farm. Cap and Spare had done well, Available and Emma had also pinned. Cam won a championship and a jumper stakes class for Teche.

As the horses were settled in for the night, it finally began to rain. I could almost hear the earth sizzle as Lockie

and I walked back to the carriage house getting soaking
wet.

9

LOCKIE LED DICE up the ramp, clipped the ties and came back out. "Do you want to go?"

"I thought I was going."

"I meant take CB and ride in with me."

"Oh. No, Mauritz wouldn't want someone like me in a session."

"What does that mean?"

"I'm a relative beginner."

"No, you're not."

"In the real world, you wouldn't take me as a student," I replied.

"I'm expensive but I can be bought," he replied.

"I'm not good enough to be at that level."

"Is that so? Here's our lesson for the day. Go get your horse and put him on the van so we can get to Balanced Rock on time."

I didn't move.

"Why are you still standing there?"

"I can't believe you're serious."

"Do I look serious?"

He did indeed.

"Yes."

"Good. You're reading the situation correctly. Go get your horse."

Cap and Emma helped gather my tack while I got CB ready, then led him from his stall.

"I'm sorry. At least it's not as warm as yesterday," I told him.

We got CB into the stall, lifted the ramp, and I climbed into the cab. Lockie shifted the van into gear and we were off.

He hadn't had a restful night's sleep. I felt him tossing and turning, even though he had to be tired. I wondered if it was his visit to jail and the impending confrontation with Nadim Anter preying on his mind. That was a question I wouldn't ask.

It wasn't out of humility or lack of self-confidence that I didn't think I was ready to ride with Mauritz. We had been working on dressage less than a year. CB was ready but I was more of a passenger than a navigator. I barely rode well enough to be a student of Lockie's as far as dressage went, he was that much more experienced than I was.

We barely said a word to each other all the way to New York. I didn't think that was a good sign.

He parked the van and shut off the engine.

"Please ask Mauritz if he's willing to have me ride in the lesson. I don't want to be rude," I said.

It was bad enough that I was going to be humiliated, I didn't want to be discourteous, too.

Lockie walked away to find Mauritz while I tacked up the horses. When the staff of the farm saw CB, they began to gather, knowing they were in for some fireworks.

A short, stocky, girl approached me. "Is that your horse?"

"Yes, it is."

"Did you buy him from Lockie?"

"No, a stable in Pennsylvania."

"I thought he was Lockie's horse."

"No, he was training him."

I felt like I was being grilled by a detective. All that was missing was a bright light shining in my eyes, and the guy running the polygraph.

"Are you riding him today?"

"Yes."

She managed not to laugh in my face.

"Well, good luck with that. I was here to see him go sideways."

"Pretty cool, huh?" I replied.

"None of us knew a horse could do that," she said, walking away.

Apparently she didn't know how to be polite, either.

I put my arms around CB's neck. "Try not to do anything that will make us need to change our identities and join the Witness Protection Program." I kissed him. "You have my assurances I will try, too."

If trying would be enough.

Lockie walked up. "You had such a thin hope that Mauritz wouldn't want you to ride in the session, but I'm sorry to tell you he is happy to see CB being ridden again."

He boosted me into the saddle, then got on Dice.

"Do you have any hints?"

"Like the Cliff Notes version of a lesson with Mauritz?"

"I'm not talking to you about this anymore," I replied as we walked the horses down the lane as our warm-up.

"Good. Tell me about the pie judging."

"Bourbon Peach Pecan won."

"Why?"

"It tasted best."

"And?"

"The crust was executed well. It was flaky, not soggy like so many of them. The baker made a very cute braid of dough on the edge and used an egg wash to make it shine. Then she added just a little bit of Turbinado sugar for sparkle and crunch."

"So she paid attention to details," Lockie said.

"Yes, she d...did."

I got what this conversation was about.

"You'll be fine and if you're not, so what? I survived him going sideways."

We rode for a while longer then turned back.

"Just before I came to the farm, I was talking to a figure skating teacher. He said ice skating was so much more difficult than riding. I said why is that? He explained that the ice is always different but horses are always the same."

"Logic from someone who has never been on a horse," I replied.

"You never know what a horse will do to you," Lockie said as we entered the indoor. "Or for you."

Mauritz Schenker was just entering from a side door and walked over to us.

"Mauritz, this is Talia Margolin," Lockie said.

"Yes, I remember. This fine fellow's owner. We'll see if he invents new gaits today."

"I hope not," I replied.

Dice got a firm pat on the neck. "*Der Harlekin.*"

"Harlequin," Lockie translated for me.

I nodded.

"Miss Margolin, ride a basic dressage test to help me understand what you need to work on."

I was going to respond but Lockie gave me a look, so I turned CB and went to the center of the arena. There was already a small audience sitting at the side.

"Take pity on me, please, Cee," I said, and closed my legs against his sides.

This was a test we had done many times, and I had seen it many more times as the Zuckerlumpens rode it every week at least once. We finished with a halt at X and then walked forward.

"I like this horse," Mauritz said.

"So do I," I replied.

"Why are you here?"

"I don't know. Lockie brought me."

Mauritz nodded. "You're here to work. But you're simply riding. Do you think he will misbehave with you?"

"No."

"Ask for more."

"Collection? Engagement?" I asked.

"From yourself."

"I'm sorry, I don't understand."

"*Vorsichtig.*" Mauritz glanced to Lockie.

"You're tentative," Lockie translated for me. "You should ride with intention."

Mauritz went into a long discussion in German while I sat there.

"He says you need to make a decision how serious you want to be. That you won't offend CB by asking him to work. We all have a job."

"If this is true, why didn't you say something?" I said to Lockie.

"I got you to this level. You are both capable of more, I've seen it. We've worked on it. This morning, you chose to revert to the mindset you had when I arrived at the farm last summer."

Mauritz smiled. "As we train the horse, we are also being trained." He pointed to his head and then his heart.

I sat there.

"Round, supple, engaged, collected," Mauritz said.

"Pay attention to the details." Lockie repeated what he had said earlier. "Do the test we worked on last. Show off."

Turning CB away, I tried to remember. Did the extended trot come before or after the half-pass? It was a jumble.

We paused at X.

"It doesn't really make a difference, does it, Cee? It was just something he invented." I closed my legs and he moved forward into the bridle. "Unless it's a real dressage test for upper level combined training. Then I'm screwed."

Not out for a hack, this time I paid attention to all the details. I asked him to lengthen the trot down the side, then returned to a working trot and made a fifteen-meter circle. We did a decent job on the corners, then I thought it was a good time to canter. I was making it up as I went along,

95

completely unable to remember anything but the few high points of what was in his test.

Riding the diagonal, we did three-stride tempi changes and didn't screw up. I felt ready to quit but realized there should be a halt, so had Cee pick up the pace for his canter down the side, then halted and reined back. We proceeded at a trot, threw in a shoulder-in, straightened, came down the centerline and halted.

I looked up. The half-pass. Skipped that totally.

"Sorry," I said.

"Gut. Very good," Mauritz said. "And no fireworks from him with her," he said to Lockie.

Lockie shrugged.

Mauritz spent the next few minutes detailing what was right and what was wrong about the test. I didn't know it was possible to drill down to that level standing that far away. There were times I had anticipated Cee, and other times he had anticipated me. The lead changes were not as straight as possible and Mauritz would have liked to see more elevation in them and throughout the ride.

Most of the commentary was aspirational in the sense that I could grow to learning and then perfecting those elements. Some of the comments pertained to my own lack of focus—not knowing what I wanted to achieve in the session.

We spent ten minutes working on my seat, hands and back to improve Cee's balance and collection.

I thanked Mauritz for his time and left the arena so Lockie could have the session he had scheduled.

We walked back down the lane, then I brought Cee back to the trailer to untack him and found a wash area outside where he could be rinsed off. As the day was getting very warm, he dried quickly and I loaded him onto the van, gave him a cookie and sat on a bucket in front of him while he worked on his hay.

Without even realizing it, tears started to course down my face.

"Talia. What are you doing?" Lockie had returned with Dice.

"You don't want to see me crying, so go away."

"I don't want to see that," he replied, came up the ramp and crouched next to me. "Why are you crying?"

"Because I'm just so used to not being good enough. Today I was."

"Sometimes the way we explain life to ourselves is wrong. You were always good enough. There is a part of you who knows that's true, yes?"

I took a breath and wiped my face. "Yes, but this—"

"You took it very seriously. It doesn't define you. It doesn't define me."

I put my arms around him and began crying again.

∽ 10 ∽

"YOU LOOK LIKE Lockie backed the van over you," Greer commented as we entered the kitchen.

Lockie studied my face. "I don't see any tread marks."

When I didn't respond, Jules came over to me. "Are you okay, Dolce?"

I nodded and started to wash my hands.

"What happened?" Greer demanded, then glared at Lockie. "If you did anything to upset her, I'll do worse to you. Count on it."

"Dial it back, Greer," Lockie replied. "She had a good ride and shocked herself."

"Can we talk about something else?" I asked.

"Your father called and will make it home for dinner. Any requests or suggestions?"

"I don't think I want lunch," I said and started for the door.

Greer followed me outside. Joly followed her. We all walked into the field where Butch and the ponies were standing in the shed, sound asleep by all appearances.

"What did he do to you?" Greer asked.

"He insisted I ride Cee for Mauritz."

"Monster," Greer commented. "I don't get it."

"I don't know why things happen the way they do. You were just better at the riding and competing than I was. You wanted it more."

"I didn't want it. I thought I would die without it."

"At some point I gave up. I did enough but couldn't do as much as you did and I wasn't willing to give up Butch the way you gave up Tea Biscuit for Sans Egal."

"And we know how well that worked out. So your point is, Talia?"

"If you don't do very much, you don't fail. And I didn't want to fail."

"All I did was fail. I never placed above Nicole Boisvert," Greer said. "She's riding jumpers now."

"There's a barn with any number of jumpers you could show," I replied.

"I want to ride Tea."

"These are the kind of things we should have known years ago but it wasn't until today when Lockie gave me no out that I understood what I had been doing."

"What does all that mean in a practical sense? Are you going to compete in dressage now?"

"Probably not. I never thought I had anything to prove and that opinion hasn't changed."

"You have your pony riders," Greer said as we turned to go back to the house."

"I want to be the kind of teacher we didn't have."

"Until Lockie."

I nodded. "He's so smart."

"Kitty Powell will be here tomorrow. She called earlier and said the mare was recuperating. She wants to pick up where they left off. With the eventing."

"I know."

"That's okay with you?"

"Remember we had a talk about Dad, my mother and your mother?"

"Can you be more specific?"

"You can't take someone away who doesn't want to go."

Kitty was an old horse show friend of both Lockie and Cam. Lockie said it was in the past and I believed him.

We walked in silence.

"There were rules I could follow in the show ring. I could know what to do," Greer said. "With Cam, I don't know."

"You know. Don't do what I did."

"What do you mean?"

"Lockie says we tell ourselves stories to make life more palatable. Sometimes we need those stories to get us through a rough patch, but when we do it to avoid what's necessary, it stops being an aid and starts being a crutch."

We stopped on the terrace.

"You think Cam is necessary to me?"

"That's for you to answer. Did you invite him to Lockie's birthday party?"

"No."

"He's Lockie's friend. If you don't I will."

Greer opened the door. "You used to be so malleable."

"Never," I replied and followed her inside.

***

Late in the afternoon, I returned from a walk in the woods with one of the new horses that wasn't in training yet. He needed a walk, and I needed time to not think.

Lockie was waiting for me when I dismounted.

"Talia, you've been very quiet this afternoon. Are you angry with me?"

"I just needed some time."

Freddi came out of the barn. "I'll take him if you want."

I handed her the reins, something I rarely did. "Thank you."

She and the horse disappeared into the barn.

We started up the driveway.

"You took a risk without having any idea how it would turn out," I said.

"And?"

"I know you so much better now."

"Is that a good thing or a bad thing?"

"I think I'm risk-adverse. You're not. It's in your nature. I must have been very difficult for you at times, trying to make you be more like me."

"This is one of your normal conversations that is completely unpredictable," Lockie said.

I looked at him. "I'm not angry. You wanted to know."

"Yes, but now I don't understand how we got to here."

"You took a chance and gave me a gift. I'm..."

"What, Tal?"

"I feel different about you now than when we left the farm this morning."

"That doesn't sound good."

"I know you've had this experience in a larger, more dramatic way than I have, but it's the emotion of it that matters. You're out on a trail and you get lost, and maybe you have to plunge through the woods, go down a cliff and over a fallen tree. It's getting dark and you wonder if you'll find your way back or if you'll spend the night out there.

Then a few minutes later, you come to the trail. You shout and pat the horse on the neck. 'Hell, yes! We made it!' It's a building block. And those little things add up over time spent together until you have a relationship that can't be duplicated. It's private, it belongs only to the two of you because it's comprised of growing trust and respect. A shared concern. Real affection. You can't buy it. You can't will it to happen. It's only created by partners sharing life."

"I once told you I was lucky."

"I remember."

"I didn't know anything about luck then."

"It's all part of the process," I replied as we walked on.

**

We had dinner, played cards, and I lost until I had enough and sat with Jules talking about pies until Lockie was ready to call it an evening. After checking on the horses, we went home. It felt like a week since that morning and I just wanted to sleep for nine hours.

"I think we disappointed the crowd at Balanced Rock today. No fireworks displays," Lockie said, turning out the light.

"Very boring. By the end of the session, they had all found something better to do."

"I need to ask this, Tal. Why does Cee go differently for you that he does for me?"

"He doesn't care that you're a better rider than I am. What he cares about is that I like him better than you do."

"I like him," Lockie protested.

"Not in the right way for him."

"He didn't even do his swish today. He was all business."

"I know!"

"It makes me think."

"Good."

"You know things I don't know."

"The reverse is true," I admitted.

"Maybe."

"Do you remember one night you told me to go to sleep and dream of the man I think you are?"

"Yes."

"You are."

Lockie dragged me closer to him. "I love it when you're completely delusional."

***

The three ponies entered the indoor arena and took the track.

I motioned for them to come over to me.

"You rode at the County Fair Horse Show and didn't place. I'm sure you're upset about it," I said.

"Why would we be?" Poppy asked.

"Because you rode very well and it would have made sense for you to win some kind of ribbon."

"Really?" Gincy looked up from one of her reins she was trying to get some soap off.

"I thought we went for the experience," Poppy said.

"You did."

"So we got experience."

"I'm really not interested in that kind of show anymore. I don't want to hurt your feelings, Talia, but I'd rather do anything else," Gincy said.

"Would you like to ride with Lockie a couple days a week?" I asked her.

Gincy's eyes grew wide, then she smiled. "Good one."

"No, I'm not teasing you. Lockie suggested it for the remainder of the summer. Then, if that's what you really want to do, you can work toward competing next year."

Gincy cheered and startled Beau.

"I don't want to ride with Lockie," Poppy said firmly. "I want to ride with you."

"You'll both ride with me, that won't change. That goes for you, too, Annie. Nothing is changing. Gincy will just have a different opportunity. We're all going to have more opportunities to do new activities this season."

"Hunting?" Annie asked.

"Yes. We've been invited to a cub hunt with the Newbury Hounds in a few weeks. There will be a hunter pace and the Halloween Parade through town."

"Yay!"

"If you have any suggestions, please let me know early in case we need to plan," I said.

"I want to ride with the field, not the Hilltoppers," Poppy said.

"Not this month. We need to find a horse for that and you'll need to put in time and effort."

"I will!" Poppy replied, practically spinning around in her saddle.

"I have no doubt about that."

We went from cheers to complete silence in a slice of a second. I turned away from the pony riders to see Lockie entering the arena.

"Talia, before you start, may I see you for one minute?"

"Sure. Everyone trot to warm-up. Independent..."

"Seat and hands," Gincy answered. "Don't pull on the reins."

"That's right."

I followed Lockie through the side door.

He used his body to push me up against the wall and kissed me, meaning it, convincing me. Then he stepped back.

"I had to do that." He turned and began walking away.

"I'm not complaining."

"I should think not."

I laughed and returned to the pony riders.

After twenty minutes of leg trembling work for them, I said they could take the short trail ride to the stream and well house that hadn't been used in fifty years.

"Walk," I reminded them. "No goofing around. If anything at all happens, I will stop trusting you and you'll have a babysitter from now until you're old enough to drive."

They looked at me in complete horror.

"Go. And I give permission for each of you to rat the others out."

"We'll be good," Gincy assured me.

I knew she would. Poppy was the one I didn't trust. She would get out of sight and gallop over Lockie's cross country course.

Just as the pony riders were leaving, Kitty's truck came down the driveway. She parked it and got out.

"Hi Talia. How are you?"

"I think the answer you'll get from everyone today is hot, but it must be hotter in Delaware."

"It was. Long drive. The truck's air conditioning gave up in New Jersey."

"Come into the house and have something cool to drink. I'm sure Jules has some exotic flavors of popsicle you can taste test. Lockie's around someplace. How's your mare?"

107

"On the mend. It'll be next year before we know how well she is."

"I'm sorry. I know you had a lot of hope for her."

"That's the way it is with horses. You might as well be playing the roulette wheel in Vegas."

I opened the kitchen door and we entered.

No Jules.

Greer was running some water into Joly's bowl.

"Where's Jules?"

"She went to town to pick up a couple things for dinner because some Italian guy called her."

I thought for a moment. "Diego called her?"

"That's who it was."

"He was at the County Fair selling spaghetti and meatball sandwiches."

Greer put the bowl on the floor. "You mean like grinders? Heroes?"

"No. He has a method where he cooks the spaghetti then presses it flat. It gets like panel. Then he cuts it and fries it."

Greer made a face.

"That's the bread. The meatballs and cheese are between these two slabs of pasta."

They looked at me in disbelief.

"It was good. I wouldn't want to eat a whole sandwich of the size he was selling, but other people would."

Greer shook her head. "What is this guy doing here?"

"He's opening up a restaurant in town called Pasta."

"Makes sense," Kitty commented.

"No, Basta," I corrected myself.

We didn't take Italian at the Briar School but we should have.

When the door opened, I expected Lockie but it was Victoria. "Hi. I'm in a bit of a predicament and need some help."

"Shock," Greer said.

"What's the problem?" I asked, hoping she didn't want Dice back.

"Tracy left."

"Where did she go?"

Victoria opened the refrigerator. "Is there any iced coffee?"

"There are coffee popsicles," Greer replied. "Not bad."

"Nursery room food," Victoria answered.

I reached for the freezer door and opened it. "Not the way Jules makes them. They probably have coffee liqueur and chocolate covered coffee beans inside, with swirls of heavy cream floating throughout." There were a half dozen popsicles in assorted colors and flavors still left from the last batch.

Victoria raised her eyebrows as I handed her the wrapped ice pop. "Thank you, Talia. Now about Tracy."

"Doesn't Greg know anyone?" Greer asked.

"Not this week," Victoria replied while carefully tasting the popsicle. Finding it to her liking, she continued to work on it. "A cup of coffee on a stick."

"Those and motorcars startle the horses," Greer replied and left the room.

"Since Emma has been spending more time here than Acadiana, maybe Freddi could split her time between us. But you should be aware that she does want to train with Lockie and now that Kitty is here, Freddi will have the opportunity."

Victoria sighed. "Where's Andrew?"

"Dad's probably working in the den."

"I'll just go say hi." Victoria walked down the hall.

As I handed Kitty a popsicle of undetermined flavor, I hoped that wasn't where Greer had gone.

11

THE DOOR OPENED and Lockie and Cam entered.

"Hi." Cam seemed genuinely pleased to see Kitty.

I was glad Greer was elsewhere. Maybe her opportunity had passed her by. Maybe it wasn't meant to be. If it was true that it wasn't possible to keep people together who wanted to be apart, maybe it wasn't possible to put them together either.

"It's going to start raining soon," Lockie said.

I tried to remember if I left any saddle pads on the fence to dry and looked up. Parti was looking in at us.

"How did he get out again?" I asked.

"He's jumping out," Lockie replied.

"He's a two-year-old," I said.

"Either that or he's become an escape artist and needs his own reality television show," Cam said, as he took the ice tea from the refrigerator and poured two glasses.. "Week One. Partial Stranger escapes from a straightjacket. Week Two. Watch Partial Stranger escape from a locked room a.k.a. stall. I think it has potential." He handed a glass to Lockie.

"We never find a gate open or the fence down," Lockie said.

"What does he want?" Kitty asked. "Give it to him."

"Yes, if he wants a chew toy. If he wants to join us for a game of cards in the dining room, no," I replied going to the door.

I had to give Parti a push in order to get to the terrace and Lockie followed me.

"Where are you going to put him?"

"A st...I don't know. I'll entertain suggestions."

We walked down the path to the driveway with the colt alongside.

"Tomorrow we call someone and have an automatic gate installed at the top of the driveway if it bothers you that he's got the run of the farm."

"You're suggesting we let him roam free?"

"I'm accepting that's what he wants to do."

"I don't believe what I'm hearing."

"It's not as though he goes anywhere. He could have gone down the road already but he comes to the house and looks in the window. This may be a behavior he'll outgrow. There is hardly a horse in the barn who can't jump over the pasture fence, but Parti's the only one who chooses to do so. I don't know how to stop him. You can't keep him in a stall permanently."

"Horses are herd animals. They want to be with other horses."

"Not this one," Lockie said. "Let's get the fence installed. We can have a keypad placed on both sides for riders. Some horses will freak for a while."

"Not Dice."

Lockie smiled. "No."

"It sounds like you have experience with them."

"The ranches where I lived in California all had them."

"What are we doing out here with him?"

"Put him in with Butch and the ponies and if he's still there later, we can turn him out with Henry."

We opened the gate and he walked inside to check out Remi who had looked up.

"Try to stay there," I called to the colt.

Lockie closed the gate and tied a lead rope around it for good measure.

"Talia, I want to talk to you about Kitty."

"Okay."

"I think I should lease Wingspread to her."

"I don't understand."

"He'll give her a good start and in a year from now she can have found something else and Wing can come back here."

"I'm not sure what's the difference. Why is a lease necessary? She'll be here."

"That's the other part. I think she should go ride with Dan Ruhlmann."

This was the first I had heard about it. "Why?"

"I've given it a good deal of thought. I'm not convinced I should be working closely with someone I had a relationship with."

I was shocked. "Do you still have feelings for her?"

"I told you we were never more than friends. So no, I don't have feelings other than I want to see her successful and happy. I'm not the right eventing trainer for her. Dan is current and he's attending the events that will help Kitty grow. There are students on the farm. No one here is interested in combined training. The business is constructed differently than ours."

"Uh huh."

"I don't think it's right to have her here and you have to deal with it, a constant reminder of my dissolute past."

I took his hand. "I don't think that about you, and I don't believe that it describes you. I'm judging you favorably. Don't work against me on it."

Lockie squeezed my hand.

"It's very sweet and I appreciate it. I would love for us to go home now but Jules went on some kind of food run so we need to be willing participants."

"Got it." He opened the door.

"Signorina Mar Go Lin," Diego called when he saw me enter the house.

It was like a tornado was cutting a swath through the kitchen and the center of it all was Diego, dicing, preparing, basting, checking on dishes in the oven, running the mixer at the same time. He was a one-man restaurant crew.

Jules was over to one side, trying to stay safely out of the way while making a salad, slicing an orange apart.

"In France they're called *suprêmes*. Because I'm Italian they're called...?"

I was supposed to answer? "I don't know."

"Segments!" Diego laughed.

"Who is this?" Lockie asked softly.

"This is Diego Something from the County Fair with the spaghetti and meatball sandwich," I replied.

"Morosoli!" Diego reminded me.

"Yes, that's it."

"We did much cooking at the restaurant, and brought it here for you. *Il terrazzo?*"

Greer grimaced as she held Joly.

"Just like my family." Diego began transporting food outside.

"I doubt it," Greer commented.

115

"This is how I learned to cook. This is what I will serve at Basta, and you will love it tonight."

My father seemed unconvinced.

"You are my pigs," Diego said.

Cam laughed.

"Guinea pigs," Jules corrected.

"Guinea? I don't know those kind of pigs. We don't have them in Italy."

Greer looked at him pityingly. "They're rodents."

My father held up a hand. "Not during a meal."

Diego glanced to Jules.

"*Roditore.*"

"*No! Impossibile!*"

"He's charming," Victoria commented.

Greer groaned loudly enough to be heard in town.

Lockie and I sat in our places. Cam and Greer sat in theirs. Diego sat on the other side of Jules.

Not including every meal prepared by Jules, this was one of the most delicious feasts I had ever had. There were thick, grilled steaks, figs stuffed with ricotta, and a hermit salad of cold potatoes, green beans, fresh tomatoes and sweet onions. Dessert was a chocolate pistachio semifreddo cake with cherry coulis.

There was very little conversation between us, just an ongoing monologue conducted by Diego, who seemed to be far less impressed by the meal than we were. If this dinner was any indication of what he would offer at Basta, the restaurant would be a success.

We sat at the table after the plates were cleared, some drinking tea, some espresso with a twist of lemon. Diego told us about his family in Italy. Of course, Victoria knew the area he described well. She said she missed Italy. Greer did not suggest her mother take the first flight back.

The restaurant, Basta, wouldn't open for business until September but there was much to do in preparation. After inviting Jules for an inspection, they had created the test dinner. Of course, Diego had a professional ice cream maker that churned a batch in seven minutes, so creating the semifreddo wasn't the investment in time it was for Jules at home.

Jules described how lovely the restaurant was—an old building of field stone and rough-hewn beams where rustic Italian food would be served. I had no trouble imagining how comfortable it would be, and so unlike going out to eat.

Lockie touched my knee under the table, so we excused ourselves and left them talking about the sunlight in Italy and the dreams Diego had of everyone having enough.

❧ 12 ❧

WHILE GREER AND I ran errands in the morning, Lockie had Kitty ride Henry and then introduced her to Wingspread. When we returned, they were on the cross country course with an audience. Lockie had obviously turned it into a group lesson with the pony riders, Cap, Emma and Cam.

"He's a wonderful instructor," I said as Greer parked the truck and we got out.

"He's a victim of his own talents," Greer replied.

"What?"

"He does too many things well. You should do...two things well."

I looked at her. "Who made that rule?"

"Because you dissipate your focus if you try to do everything at the same time."

"What if he's one of the unusual people who can manage it?"

"The rules apply to everyone."

There was no point in arguing with her.

"You'll be relieved to know that will be changing. We've talked about training horses and riders," I said.

"Is that enough for him?"

"He'll be whipping for the Newbury Hounds. So there you have two."

"Maybe one should be showing."

I looked across the field and saw Lockie addressing the group. "It's his choice."

We started to the house.

"It was surprisingly easy to let showing fall away. I don't miss being judged," Greer replied.

"That was the worst. Or was it getting up at three in the morning? Lockie gets something positive from it. I still haven't figured out what."

"Do you two ever argue?"

"Of course."

"How do you get past it?"

"We mutually give in."

The door opened and Joly rushed out to greet us.

***

I had Poppy get up on Knock Knock for a short session while Lockie put Gincy up on Call to do a little basic dressage. While she had overcome most of her concerns about riding at speed across country, that was still not Gincy's favorite activity. Not there to force any rider to do what they didn't want to do, rather we wanted to help them achieve their goals. Poppy enjoyed adventure and excitement. Gincy preferred quiet precision.

Cap watched Poppy and Annie trot around the ring. "Knock's a nice pony even if he has some soundness issues."

Dina had been very upfront about the pony and had left us with his latest radiographs. He would be serviceably sound with light work, but he'd never return to the heavy showing schedule he had once been on.

We were fine with that and there was an enormous amount he could teach our riders. Greer had ridden him briefly and there didn't seem to be anything Knock didn't know. Besides that, he was a sweetheart, gentle and sensible. This would be a change for Poppy since Tango's personality was more like her own, high energy, enthusiastic about going forward.

Today's lesson was more about keeping the pony going than having to worry about him getting away from her. I didn't want to see her resorting to leg aids in an attempt to replicate the way Tango went. The girls needed to understand that each horse they rode would be different and it was their job to make it shine.

"Don't be frustrated with him, Poppy. That's his normal speed. Push him up to the bridle but don't nag him."

"He's not going fast enough," she replied.

"For what purpose?" I asked.

"For anything. For the lesson."

"He's fine. You're the one with the problem."

"I'm using my legs."

Cappy leaned over to me. "He's only got two speeds and the next one is slower than this."

"He's a show ring hunter. That's the speed he knows."

Poppy turned to me. "Why can't we go a little faster?"

"Learn to ride him at this speed and then go faster. All I see is a rider struggling. Why am I seeing that?"

"Because I'm struggling to keep him going."

"He's not a wind-up toy. He'll keep going. Pay attention to what you're supposed to be doing."

"Eh! Can I go get Tango?"

"No."

"Maybe I need spurs."

"No, you don't. You don't have control enough over your legs to wear spurs."

"A stick?"

"We don't beat our horses or riders at Bittersweet Farm. We work with them."

And so it went for twenty minutes. Knock had his speed and Poppy was so distracted by it that she was well beyond glowing at the end of the lesson.

As we left the ring, Lockie and Gincy walked through the yard. So pleased with herself, she was grinning. I loved seeing that, as there had been quite a few days when things hadn't gone as well for her.

The girls went out for a short walk in the woods and Lockie and I went into the barn to get the next horses on our to-be-ridden list.

***

Late the following afternoon, the commercial horse transport came for Wingspread. Kitty had spent hours packing all his clothes, his tack and hers, then preparing him for the trip to Kentucky during the cool of the night. She would be following the entire way.

I was impressed by her commitment to Wing but seeing the trailer pull up the driveway and turn left for town, and eventually the highway, was predictably a tough moment.

"What's wrong, Tal?" Lockie asked as he turned to the barn to finish the day's work.

It was best just to say the words. "I got him back for you and now you're giving him away."

"Silly. That's not how it is. Wing's an event horse with no job. He needs a rider, and Kitty is a very good one. They'll be training with one of the finest eventers in the country—and he'll come back. The gift you gave me was more than a horse. That can't go down the road."

I shrugged instead of having a big dramatic moment.

"Or are you just upset by Wing leaving even though I'm staying?"

"Why can't I have both?"

Lockie laughed as he put his arm around me. "Because we're not going to become hoarders and wind up on the news portrayed as Sad Act Farm with a hundred and fifteen horses, plus a couple donkeys."

We began to walk inside.

"What happens when Wing comes home? What's his job then?"

"Not a fortune teller. I know we have two appointments tomorrow morning. If you can turn your lessons over to Greer, that would be good."

Cee had his head over his stall door waiting for me to do something about turning him out. I gave him a disk of carrot from my pocket.

"Who's coming?" I asked.

"Both want training board. Cam and I met them at Long River. Good amateur riders but neither of them are happy where they are. They've heard about our program—"

"We have a program?"

"We sure do, and they're interested."

"What do we do that no one else does?"

"I wouldn't characterize it as no one," Lockie replied. "How many people really want their trainer to be standing in the middle of the ring shouting 'I can't believe I'm seeing this! No! No! No!' By the time you're an adult, you want to be treated as one."

"They don't like that?" I asked. "That was the best part for Greer and me. Get humiliated then she'd go out to party and I'd eat ice cream while plotting my getaway."

"Did you really?"

"Yes."

"I'm sorry I wasn't here."

I laughed. "You wouldn't have liked me very much then."

He tilted his head considering it. "Probably true."

"You're bad," I said.

"Bad enough to get myself arrested."

"What are we going to do about it?"

Lockie walked to the tack room. "I have a court date and your father called his lawyer. Sometime next month, I'll get in front of the judge and tell the truth that Mr. Anter stumbled and fell upon me. As I tried to right him, he mistakenly interpreted that as an assault."

I followed him. "Is that what happened?"

"That's my story and I'm sticking to it. Am I going to say the man hates me because he thinks I behaved inappropriately with his then underage daughter? There's her reputation to consider. That doesn't need to be in a court document for all to see."

"What if he says you're lying?"

"Of course he will. He didn't amass a fortune by being a nice man."

"It's possible to run a business and be ethical."

"I see your father do it every day. Nadim should take lessons from him," Lockie replied. "Do not worry about this. It's a nothing little thing."

"Have you ever been arrested before?"

"No, I always got away with it." Lockie started to laugh.

"Yes, it's very funny."

"It was. Someone set up a hot tub in the stable yard of one of the venues on the Winter Circuit."

"How old were you?"

"Seventeen?"

"Go on." I didn't want to hear but now that he started, he had to finish.

"It was about midnight. There were adult beverages. There were adult candies. The girls were squealing. The boys were being boys. Clothes were optional. And the cops came. We explained it idiotically, I'm sure, but that was hardly the most pressing activity they could check on so they left."

"Without sounding judgmental, how do you carouse half the night and ride the next day?"

"Talia, when you're a seventeen year old boy, you are invincible. Where do you think the idea for Superman came from?"

"When you had your accident–"

"No," Lockie interrupted me. "No, by that time in my life, I wasn't a kid anymore. I had seen too much to think there was such a thing as invincibility."

"I have to ask."

"You don't. It was a judgment call. No one reported that the course was going sour. It was muddy but sometimes courses are. We've got sausage. You can't crank the handle in reverse and get a pig."

"I want this to not have happened to you."

"Really? Then I wouldn't be here."

"We don't know that," I replied.

"I don't know why I would have returned to training equitation riders when I had a three-star horse."

That was true but it meant that in some way I had to be grateful for the accident that nearly killed him. "I want you to never have suffered," I said.

"I want the same for you, Silly." He kissed me. "Let's do something tonight."

126

"What? Throw caution to the wind and watch *Downton Abbey*?"

"You're making fun of my entertainment choices," Lockie replied.

"Why, yes, I am."

He snuggled at my neck. "What did you dream you would do with your boyfriend?"

"I never thought about having a boyfriend," I answered honestly.

"We'll have to rectify that. Is there a puppet show in town?" he asked.

"What?"

❧ 13 ❧

THE SKY WAS OVERCAST, the day muggy, and the temperature already climbing as Greer and I were finishing a late breakfast on the terrace. In this heat, Joly didn't even want to play with the frogs and Parti was grazing lazily on the lawn twenty-five feet away from us. He was free to come and go as he pleased since he'd get out anyway. The electric gate company would be visiting next week.

"What kind of lesson do you want for the Glitter Girls?"

"Equitation," I replied.

"Why?"

"You're a wonderful eq rider."

"Debatable, but why would these pony hunter riders need equitation?"

"Because everyone requires a good, solid foundation. Their position must be correct to do anything of value."

"I didn't think of it like that."

I heard a truck stop. "UPS man."

"Lockie's birthday present?"

"It better be."

Tom appeared on the walk, carrying two boxes.

I breathed a sigh of relief as I stood. "I hope those are for me."

"Yes, they are."

I signed and he handed them to me.

Jules came out of the house with a little decorative bag containing two muffins. "For the road," she said.

"You make this my favorite stop," he replied. "Thank you. See you next week."

I put the boxes on the table, removed the utility knife from my pocket, and opened the first one. After digging through all the packing material, I found the small tube, removed the lid and tipped it over.

Out slid the most beautiful fountain pen I had ever seen.

"Geez, Tal," Greer exclaimed.

"It's gorgeous," Jules said.

It had been custom-made to my specifications of dark green and red celluloid.

Jules put the tip of her finger lightly on the gold hunting whip. "What's the clip made from?"

"A vintage stock pin Victoria found and Shawn took it apart and made it work. At first, he did think it was a strange request but after he put it all together, I got a note from him saying how well it came out."

I unscrewed the cap and we could see the vintage gold nib, polished and shiny as though it was brand new.

"Will Lockie use this?" Jules asked.

"He's been keeping a journal since his accident. Yes, I think having a beautiful pen will be something he will enjoy."

"May I?" Greer asked, knife poised above the packing tape on the other box.

"Of course."

A moment later, Greer extracted a bottle of ink from the box and managed to tear and cut off the protective wrapper. What was revealed was a bottle of ink.

"Is this custom-made, too?"

"Practically. It's made in Konrad's kitchen in Poland. Small batches."

Greer opened the bottle and I dipped the nib into the ink. She pushed a pad of paper she had been making notes on toward me and I wrote Bittersweet Farm as neatly as my handwriting would allow.

"Beautiful!"

"I hope he likes it," I said.

Jules gave me a hug. "He will love it."

I wanted Lockie to use and enjoy the pen, but more than that to know I thought the accident was no longer a disaster. It was something that would always leave me ambivalent because he had suffered, and it had taken away the life he had known. In recompense, the crash with Wing had given him a life with us. The accident had been a gift to me, to all of us.

Lockie had been right. He seemed to be able to accept life's curve balls a bit more easily than I did, but I was educable.

Cam's truck stopped at the path so I quickly headed for the pantry as Lockie and Cam got out and started toward the house.

"Just the handsome man I want to see," Jules said.

"You don't have to wait for me to show up, I'll always be available to you, Jules," Cam replied.

"What a smooth talker." Jules lifted the napkin covering the basket of morning buns.

"Oh no, I couldn't." Cam sat and pulled the basket closer. "Maybe just the one. And a cup of coffee."

Jules smiled. "And you'll be here for lunch."

"Naturally." He turned to Greer. "Good morning, Gracie. You look lovely today."

She was stunned into silence.

Lockie grabbed for a bun. "Our ladies will be here any time now, Tal."

"I'm ready."

"Wait, before you go," Jules said to him. "It's your birthday this week and we always—"

"—overdo it," Greer interjected.

"No. Well, yes, we do, but it is a special day so we're allowed. Most of the time I make the birthday dinner but this year, Diego has offered to let us have the dinner at the restaurant—"

"—as a test run, no doubt," Greer got in.

"Only if you would enjoy having dinner there. Of course, that way, there is already space, tables and chairs for as many guests as you'd like to invite," Jules pointed out.

Lockie took a bite of the bun and looked at me.

"Your choice," I said.

"If it's easier for you, Jules, that's fine with me," he said.

"Diego can still make whatever you'd like. Obviously. You're the birthday boy."

Lockie tried to wipe the sugar from his mouth with fingers covered in sugar. "We could invite Sibby and Day."

I reached for a napkin. "And Greg, and the pony riders."

"The Swope grandparents," Greer said.

"My parents. Am I invited?" Cam asked.

"You were invited already," I reminded him.

"That's right."

"Yes, your parents and Kerwin."

"The Meades," Greer added. "And Sassy and Ethan."

"We do want the police on our side given our proclivities for getting into legal trouble," Lockie agreed.

"If this is sounding too much like a crowd, we can just have dinner here," I said to Lockie.

"It's fine. We eat together every day. We can be wildly sociably for one evening," he replied, taking my hand and leading me down the path.

We hadn't been at the barn for five minutes when an SUV pulled into the yard and parked next to my truck. Two women got out and walked up to us.

"Hi. Let's see if I remember," said Lockie. "Joan Schultz, this is Talia Margolin, the other trainer at the farm."

I shook hands with her.

"And...Sandy Atkinson, this is Talia, who grew up here."

"Hi, Talia," Sandy said as she gave my hand a firm shake.

"We can take a walk around and show you the two barns. We have an indoor that we seem to use all year long. We have the outdoor arena and a cross country course."

"Miles of trails we use for conditioning and relaxation. Every horse takes a walk after work," I added.

"Our training sessions are short because neither science nor I have had it demonstrated that more is more. More is less when it comes to a horse. You choose what you want to work on for the session, have it confirmed and quit.

Progress comes in small increments. If you don't go backwards by pushing, you're always ahead."

"To stay in condition, don't horses and riders need more work than that a day?" Joan asked.

"Yes," I replied. "That's why we rely on our trails so much. If you go up and down those hills without stirrups, you'll be tired when you get back and when you can walk again, stronger."

The women laughed.

"We have very few rules," I said. "No crops, no spurs, no over-bitting, no lunging as a standard routine. No drugs, no drinking."

Lockie nodded. "Unless it's the end of the day and I share an ale with Talia's horse."

"The horse drinks with you?" Joan asked.

"He has to. The pub won't let CB in since he's underage," Lockie replied.

"Do you have room for us?" Sandy asked.

I glanced at Lockie.

"This is a decision you might want to mull over," he said.

"Have a lesson," I said.

"We have our tack with us," Joan said. "Do you have any horses we could ride?"

I laughed. "I think we can find some."

"Wonderful."

I heard hoof beats behind me and a moment later, Parti stuck himself between Lockie and me.

The women jumped back, startled.

"You're going to scare people by doing that," I told him and reached in my pocket for a slice of carrot. "This is my sister's colt. He is supposed to be in but he's something of a free spirit and gets out. He never goes anywhere, so we don't worry about it."

Lockie gave him a firm pat on the neck. "And next week we're getting an electric gate."

"I love it here," Joan said. "This is more than we thought we'd be able to find."

"If it's like home then the—"

"The top trainers are going to be at the top barns where everything is business," Sandy finished. "It's not easy to find a good trainer who isn't trying to be the star of the Grand Prix ring."

I nodded. "Lockie has that tee-shirt."

He laughed.

"We did our research," Joan assured me.

"Everything lives forever on the Internet," I replied.

"We made some calls, too," Sandy said.

"I'll have to delete my secrets," Lockie replied.

"We didn't find them." Joan smiled.

Lockie breathed a sigh of relief. "That net detective cost as much as a good prospect. I'm glad to know it was worth it."

"Where's the paperwork?" Sandy asked.

"You'll ride. You'll go home and think about it. Tomorrow you can call and give me your decision."

Sandy looked at Joan. "I've never met anyone in this business who was so unwilling to take our money."

We got the two women up on Keynote and Bijou within a few minutes, then walked to the indoor.

Greer texted me to come to the house immediately, so I left Cap with Lockie, then went to find out what the huge emergency was.

"The lawyer is calling you," Jules said as I entered the kitchen.

"I hope that's our lawyer."

"Yes, he wants your version of the story."

"My version? A.K.A. the truth?"

"That's what lawyers do. They're naturally nosy and ask a lot of questions. This time it's a friendly. The next lawyer it won't go so easy," Greer commented.

"You mean Paul Gish's lawyer is going to try to burn me at the stake."

"That's his job."

"Paul Gish should come here and say these things to my face! But he won't because he's a coward."

"Please don't get any ideas, Tal," Jules said quickly.

"I should go to the studio. Embarrass him in front of all his co-workers the way he's trying to humiliate me. That's fair. Why should he be able to attack me and I can't attack him in return?"

Jules handed me a cup of tea. "You're defending yourself by having a lawyer and presenting yourself as a civilized lady."

"I don't care about civilized when someone is trying to do real harm to me."

Greer shook her head.

"You're taking this pretty calmly," I said to her.

"Of course, it's not happening to me," Greer replied.

I was surprised at how quickly I became angry with her. This was the old Greer. This was the same kind of situation we had been through countless times in the past. She could adopt an air of superiority that set me on edge and had always made me want to push her into the nearest pile of steaming manure.

My reaction was a reminder that my sister wasn't my enemy. "I'm glad it's not," I said, honestly.

"Do you want me to sit next to you when you're on the phone?"

"I would love it," I replied as the phone began ringing.

We went to the den and I picked up the phone. It was a tolerably brief conversation, in which I reiterated my side of the story. The lawyer thanked me and hung up.

"I don't know how you go about proving or disproving my culpability in Ami Gish's fall."

"You've seen Asher Lau's show on TV, *Legal Brief*. They call experts as witnesses. They'd pay George Morris a couple thousand dollars for his time, and he'd get on the stand and say you're not supposed to flop around in the saddle like a rag doll."

"Then the Gish attorney would call Ami to the stand and she'd hobble up pathetically and say I confused her and now her leg is broken," I said. "Permanently. She'll never walk normal again."

"What are you talking about?"

"That's what they say on the wrestling shows Lockie watches."

Greer grimaced. "Ami will be fine. Her father just thinks they've hit the lottery."

"They've hit a speed bump more like," I replied.

"Talia," Lockie called from the kitchen.

"What now?" Greer asked as we made our way through the house.

14

JULES WAS WRAPPING ICE in a towel and Gincy was holding Annie's hand while blood dripped from her nose.

"What happened? Did she fall off?" I asked.

"Lean forward," Greer said.

"It's our fault," Poppy confessed.

"It was an accident," Lockie said. "They were running across the field playing tag with Parti, and Annie tripped. I don't have to be a medical professional to know that nose is broken."

"Cool!" Poppy exclaimed.

Joly was dashing around the room barking.

Jules pressed the ice to Annie's face.

"Did someone call her mother? Should we take her to the hospital?" Greer asked.

"Mrs. Zakarian's on the way," Lockie answered.

"No more playing tag with the colt," I said.

"He wanted to. He came up to us and nudged us," Gincy explained.

"What if he caught you?"

"He did, but he just tagged us and then we were it and chased him."

"Is this something that's done?" Jules asked.

"No. He's such a bad influence on you girls. Don't do it again."

"Next time he'll want to be pushed on the swings," Lockie commented as he opened the refrigerator searching for something to eat.

"I have lunch for everyone. Go sit down," Jules said and handed him a piece of cheese. "It'll be right there. We have a small emergency in progress."

"I understand but I have a lesson at one," Lockie replied.

"Greer, please get him something to drink, and a roll," I suggested.

"Everything's in the refrigerator." Jules removed the bloody towel from Annie's nose and exchanged it for a fresh one.

"Shhh," Greer told Joly as she got the platter of sandwiches and fresh bread and butter pickles Jules had made just two hours ago.

Cam came into the kitchen. "Lunchtime? And someone's been in a fight. I hope you got a good shot in," he said to Annie.

"That colt of yours persuaded them to play tag with him."

"Your colt," he reminded Greer.

"Luckily she didn't fall on the aisle," Jules commented.

If that had been the case, she could have knocked out a couple teeth and her mother would have real reason to be unhappy. This was bad enough. Unfortunately, life was not a risk-free activity and it was just as easy to get hurt crossing the street as it was crossing the field. Add a horse to the equation and the risk increases.

I was willing to take the risk but not willing to be foolish. That set-point was different for everyone. Lockie wasn't a risk-taker but there were choices I wished he didn't make. It would be dishonest to say I wasn't relieved he had decided to stop showing jumpers the way he had in Florida.

"Come on, Talia." Lockie motioned to me as he went to the terrace. "Eat."

***

Day had finally returned from their fishing expedition in Canada with her grandmother, Sibby, and then she'd taken some time to do art work for a few local organizations. This was the first time I'd seen her in August and thought she looked fresh and fit. Since the hunting season was starting for the Jamiesons, it was good Day was ready for it.

"Is it me, Lockie, or is Moonie strong?" Day asked after they had gone around the ring at a very enthusiastic canter.

"You're right. Did you have anyone ride him while you were away?"

Because Day had talked herself into thinking Sibby's horse needed company, she had chosen to leave Moonie at home, instead of his usual stall at Bittersweet. That meant he also had a vacation.

"No. My cousin promised me she would but she went to Nantucket."

"It's not a problem. He's a young horse and feeling a bit fresh."

Good for Moondust. It was hot and the air was so heavy with humidity that wringing a handful out like a sponge didn't seem impossible.

"Let's set up a gymnastic that will encourage him to slow down."

Lockie had me help him create a circular pattern with ground poles at the twelve, five and eight o'clock positions. At the six o'clock there were four poles leading in or out of the gymnastic.

142

"You're going to trot straight in and either make a right or left turn. Go around the circle and then trot out. If a horse sees a straight line and is feeling sharp, he can increase his speed as he goes. This exercise breaks that direct route. You still have to ride him but Moonie's smart and I'm sure he'll figure it out."

"Would it be beneficial to gallop him up the hill first?"

"I'm sure that would take the edge off but it's not a training method. Moonie needs to understand that his job is to cooperate with your requests no matter how he feels. If he does that, that's trained. If you run him until he's tired, then he's learned nothing."

"I get it. In our family, a good gallop solves just about every problem."

"It won't solve this, so trot our teenager over the first poles, go left, inside leg, inside rein. Sit back, don't lean into his desire to rush forward. Legs at the girth, trot the circle and then exit. Try to maintain the same pace throughout."

The first time, Moonie stepped on three rails and took a huge leap over the last one. Day, who I considered a good rider, had difficulty trotting the circle and exiting.

"That's so embarrassing," she exclaimed as Moonie stopped.

"I've seen much worse. Try it again. Shoulders back, feet a little forward of where yours are. Don't fight. He doesn't understand what's expected of him."

"How can he not understand? It's not as though he's never been ridden over a gymnastic before."

"They have good memories," Lockie admitted, "but they also have powerful emotions. He wants to play. It's your job to convince him that for the twenty minutes he's here, it's not playtime. Go again."

If the second attempt was better, I couldn't detect the improvement.

"Be quiet. Don't anticipate. What he does shouldn't change how you're going to ride."

"That would be like saying the car is sliding on the ice, just let it happen," Day replied.

"Not at all. You are the only reference point he has. If you change your behavior, he's confused. Ride past his antics. Be steady. If he's unpredictable, you have to be predictable. Your attitude should be that you don't care what he does."

Day shook her head as she aimed Moonie for the gymnastic.

"Shoulders back," Lockie said.

This effort was better than the last two.

"Try it again. Go to the right this time."

By staying centered and quiet, maintaining light but firm contact, Day got Moonie around with a limited amount of scrambling. The next round was better. Then they got it right.

"Do the exact same thing one more time and you're done for the day."

Moonie trotted smartly around the circle, exited and halted in front of Lockie.

"Very nice. Remember, you're not on a field hunter. He's a young horse that was destined for the hunter ring so Moonie doesn't have the disposition you're accustomed to now. Maybe in a few years he will but you have a lot of work to do and he has to grow up emotionally."

"You wouldn't recommend that I hunt him this season," Day said.

"I think he'll be confused. Moonie needs to go back a few steps to quiet work. You can take him out and have a canter by himself, or with the group, but if he gets excited, you need to adjust the program for him. Having the field galloping around him is not going to help."

"Okay." Day patted his neck. "I can take him for a walk now?"

"Sure. Have a good time," Lockie replied and we watched the two of them walk away.

"Most other trainers would have said sure, hunt him, show him, have a blast," I said as we walked to the barn.

"She has options some riders don't. Day is patient and there are other horses for her to ride, here or at home. Moonie is a nice horse and there's no sense in spoiling him before his career begins. Take a year of quiet work now and he'll be Mr. Cool later. Otherwise, he'll always have quirks difficult to resolve."

"Is that what you would say about CB?"

"What would you say?" Lockie asked.

"Yes."

"So would I."

"What can we do to make life better for him?"

"You can't be serious, Tal. His every need is catered to, he has someone who adores him, and only once in a while do I get on and spoil his day."

I didn't reply.

"Do you want me to stop riding him?"

"No. I want you both to be happy and reaching your fullest potential. Is that too much?"

Lockie put his arm around me. "A man's reach should exceed his grasp—"

"Or what's a heaven for?" I finished the Robert Browning quote.

He laughed. "You did learn something in that expensive prep school you didn't graduate from."

"The answer's yes, then."

"No. It's an aspiration. Maybe you're the rider CB really wants to work for."

I sighed. "I think I should ride him in the Newbury Hunt Club show next month."

"Why?"

I thought for a moment. "Publicity."

"Don't make choices based on Paul Gish's lawsuit. Show him if you want to, not because you think it will counteract all the rumors going around about how mean you are."

I stopped on the path. "What have you heard?"

"Silly. I was teasing you. I haven't heard anything. You know Robert Easton is running his mouth, but he always has. It'll blow over in a few months. Ami will return to school, people will forget her except as some girl who couldn't stay on one of the best ponies in the state. Am I right?"

"I suppose."

"That's the wrong answer."

"You're right."

"I love being right."

***

Late in the afternoon, I took Poppy and Gincy for a walk to the end of the road and then onto an old logging trail they had never been on.

"Is Annie going to be okay?" Gincy asked as we entered the woods.

"She'll breathe through her mouth for a few days but other than swelling and a bruise, she'll be fine."

"Are we still going out with the Newbury Hounds this month?" Poppy asked.

"Yes, if you want to."

"Can I ride one of the horses?"

"The question is phrased, 'May I ride one of the horses?'"

"Why?"

"Because you certainly have the ability to ride most of the horses at the barn but whether I will let you do so is the question." I brushed at a fly trying to sit on Cee.

"Will you let me?"

"No, not this time. You may ride Call but you'll still be in with the Hilltoppers."

Poppy practically stomped her foot in her iron. "Why?"

"Because you had trouble riding Beau."

"Are you going to hold that against me?"

"I'm using it as a measurement of how much further you need to go before you're ready to move up to the next level. I'm almost sure you could stay on but being almost convinced is not enough. You need to be in control of your body so you don't bang the horse in the mouth with each landing, or pass Sibby Jamieson as everyone is galloping with the hounds."

"Tell me what I have to do and I'll do it," Poppy said plaintively.

I thought for a moment, knowing how much this meant to her and also knowing how important it was that I keep her safe from herself. "Ride better. You're very good on Tango but when I rode the hunter pace last year, one fence Lockie and I took was taller than Tango. The hunt can't stop and solve your issues, that's not fair to them and I fully expect something like that would happen. When you're stronger and more knowledgeable, you can ride with the field. Until then, it's not safe."

"Give it a rest, Poppy," Gincy said, most surprisingly.

"Let's be nice. Why do you want to ride with the field?" I asked.

Poppy didn't answer.

"Tell her," Gincy said.

"It seems like more fun," Poppy replied, unconvincingly.

Gincy urged Beau closer to me. "The girls on the Internet have been saying things and Poppy wants to prove them wrong."

"What girls," I asked, even though I had a strong suspicion.

"The Easton riders."

"Whatever forum or site it is, don't go there anymore. That's Number Two."

Gincy looked at me in confusion. "What's Number One?"

"We don't use our horses to boost our egos, or to prove anything to anyone. We know that, don't we?"

"Yes, Talia," Gincy said.

"Poppy?"

"They're talking smack about you," Poppy protested. "I want to show them you're a great teacher. Greater than Voldemort Easton."

I tried not to laugh. "If I'm not upset, you don't need to be upset for me and leap to my defense. It really doesn't make a difference to our lives. Some people will always be unkind. Think how unhappy they must be."

Gincy nodded.

Poppy wasn't so easily swayed by reason. She cared about me and, in her eyes, I had been wronged.

15

"LOCKIE, Robert Easton is talking about me."

"So I've heard."

It was nearly dark on our terrace. The workday was finally over. Everyone had eaten, everyone was where they should be and we were sitting outside waiting for the rain to begin.

"You didn't tell me?" I asked

"I forgot. It wasn't that important."

"Maybe not to you but Poppy is upset."

"Kick the can to her mother."

"She wants to prove to the mean girls that I'm a good instructor."

"Give her something else to think about. Turn her head in the opposite direction from the flapping plastic bag."

"In a way, you're right," I said.

"In what way am I wrong?"

"This is not fatal. We will all survive the Paul Gish Incident as it will come to be known."

"Yes…"

"But we all have an emotional component, too. We don't always make sense, sometimes we overreact but it's also a real, and undeniable, part of life."

"Here's the deal. I'm willing to be right there for you, but everyone else has to find their own Lockie. Emotions in people and horses are transitory. You ride through them. It's not my job to hold the hand of anyone who rides here except you. And possibly Greer."

I thought about it for a minute. "Can we both be right?"

"If you think about it, there is no way to make Poppy feel better about the situation. Give her the human equivalent of a pat on the neck and then urge her forward."

"She's a child."

"A pat and a cookie then."

"I want to do the right thing."

"Do the best you can, that's all you should ask of yourself."

I felt the first raindrop on my arm. A moment later, the sky split apart with a streak of lightning and we were drenched.

***

First thing the next morning, Sandy and Joan brought their horses to the barn and signed the training contract. They were so happy.

They were so happy that Cap and I found it odd and wondered what had happened to cause giving us a good chunk of money a month made them so delirious they had required a celebratory coffee before their first session.

"If they were riding with anyone like Rui," I said as I got CB's bridle off its rack, "then it's understandable."

"He was that bad?"

"I could never fully describe just how awful and how he wrecked that couch."

Cap leaned against the manure fork. "Was he using it as a trampoline?"

"That's as good an explanation as any other we've come up with."

"I rode with Nancy Johnson who was good for the basics. She was going to UConn, then graduated and left town."

"It wasn't traumatic?" I asked.

"No."

"You didn't cry?"

Cap shook her head.

"Did she yell at you? Humiliate you? Taunt you?"

"No. No. No."

"Then how can you say you had riding lessons?" I laughed.

"The instructor at the Country Day School in California was okay. When the surf wasn't up."

"Are you kidding me?"

"No, he had a surfboard on the top of his pick-up. When the waves are waving, you have to heed their siren call."

"You're making it up."

"I'm not. He got fired the year after I left because there was a huge wave forming so that everyone was going to Hawaii to catch it. I'll bet Lockie knows all about this," Cap said.

"What do I know about?" Coming up beside me, he put his arm around my shoulders.

"Surfing."

"Not my sport. Is CB ready to ride?"

"Just about."

"Meet me in the indoor," he said and left the barn.

Cap helped me tack him, and stood by while I got on. We walked to the ring and for the next twenty minutes Cee and I worked on me learning how to more effectively engage his hindquarters.

***

Just before afternoon chores began, Greer returned from Basta where Jules had been cooking for most of the day. It had been Greer's task to set the tables because that was one of her special talents, probably inherited from her mother, but I wasn't going to say that.

"It looks fantastic," she said, "and the aromas are better than that."

"When do we have to be there?" I threw hay to Call.

"The invitations were for six-thirty so you don't have tons of time. What kind of help do you need?"

"Check the schedule and pick anything. Cap figured it all out so we wouldn't be leading horses to the pasture in our dresses."

"Have you decided what you're going to wear?" Greer called as she went down the aisle.

"Jules's purple dress."

"You wore than last year."

"I know and Lockie likes it. I don't wear dresses often enough to need a new one for every occasion."

"What's he wearing?"

"He has a sport coat from Florida, which he'll remove immediately, and navy trousers with a plaid shirt."

I hoped this wasn't going to be too much of a celebration as the list of people we needed to invite seemed to grow with the space we suddenly could fill by having it at Basta instead of our dining room. Lockie's friends and business acquaintances would be there, but no one from my father's business or political circle. Greer and I had been disappointed to learn that my grandparents were on a cruise to Alaska so had no way to make it.

"When are you going to give him the pen?"

"After the party. I don't want to risk misplacing it."

"There shouldn't be any presents," Greer replied.

At Lockie's request, we had asked people donate to the local shelter in place of getting him something but I seriously doubted that guests wouldn't bring him a gift. Greer had gotten him new breeches, Jules and my father had asked Day to paint him on horseback—but she refused to tell us on what horse or where.

There were only the four of us, because the Zuckerlumpens had to go home to change and bring both sets of parents to the restaurant. Freddi was over at Victoria's helping there, and she was getting a ride with them. Cam was going from Acadiana to home to pick up Kate, Fitch and Kerwin. Pavel, Danuta and Tomasz had to clean up, too. Even with superior organization, we were late finishing, and raced to our respective showers without wasting a second.

"You're making too much of a fuss over me," Lockie said as I finished in the bathroom.

"Why do you say that?"

"So many people, all this rushing around."

"These are friends and acquaintances. They all want to celebrate."

"Everyone likes a party."

It didn't seem as though he was part of the group he called "everyone." "It's a celebration in your honor. How lucky we all are that you were born. That day is special to us because of you. It's not a random get-together."

He turned away to his jacket.

"Have you never had a party for your birthday?"

"Yes, but not like this."

"If you feel uncomfortable, you can go home at any time."

He sat on the edge of the bed for a minute, then stood to go into the bathroom. When he returned, I was ready to go.

"I always liked that dress," Lockie said.

"I'm wearing it for you."

Wasn't that obvious?

"The good part about tonight is we wind up back here."

I nodded. "The best present ever."

Lockie took my hand and we went to the party that seemed to baffle him.

There were several cars in the Basta parking lot and since everyone I knew drove a truck most of the time, it would be a surprise to see who had already arrived. I parked next to my father's car and we got out.

The main building was old, but there had been several additions over the years where fieldstones hadn't been used. This part of Connecticut was built on rock and those had been put to as much use as possible by farmers. Lights lit the way to the hand-hewn door and that opened to an enclosed sunroom of stones and beams. There were pots of flowers blooming, greenery and bunting in Bittersweet Farm's stable colors.

When we entered the main room, the scents of Italian food floated temptingly in the air around us. It reminded me how many hours it had been since I had eaten last.

"You finally got here," Greer said, approaching us. "Happy Birthday, Lockie." She gave him a hug and a kiss on the cheek. "Dad's getting a guided tour from Diego. Does he ever get tired?"

"Not that I've seen," I replied.

"We're at the big table, and everyone else will just have to come visit if they want to talk to one of us. I can't imagine why anyone would leave food on the table. I tasted the cold marinated eggplant. It's his family's recipe. We're stealing it because it's so good."

It took us five minutes to get to the table where my father was deep in a conversation with Pavel about the electric gate, not seeming very happy about it.

"Hi," I said.

Lockie pulled out a chair for me, then sat in the one next to it.

"Hi. I hope we eat soon, I skipped lunch," my father said. "Not on purpose. By the time I remembered it was too late."

"Where's Jules?"

"Where do you think?"

"The kitchen." I turned. "I'll see if I can pry her out of there. She must be in her good clothes."

"She is."

I looked around and spotted the door. "I'll be right back."

"It's a black hole. You enter and wind up on the other side of the universe," Lockie replied.

"No space travel tonight."

Greeting people along the way, it took me another five minutes just to get across the room. I opened the kitchen door and went inside. Jules was overseeing a couple of line cooks and the sous chef while Diego was putting the finishing touches on antipasto platters. The amount of food seemed enough for a banquet.

"Hey!" Jules called out. "Is everyone looking for me?"

"Yes. You're supposed to have the night off."

Diego laughed.

She untied an apron, removed it and picked up a platter. "Get the other one, please."

"I have to serve tonight?"

"He hasn't hired wait staff yet."

I gave Diego a stern look.

"It'll be family style," Jules explained.

"How is that possible with all the tables?"

"We'll manage," she replied confidently.

I foresaw an evening in which Greer and I barely got a chance to sit down before jumping up for more food.

"Maybe we should make this buffet style," I suggested.

If people could serve themselves, they could be human jack-in-the-boxes and not me.

"We'll see." Jules expertly wielded the platter the size of a flying saucer into the dining room.

"Here, let me help," Aly Beck offered, taking the platter from me. "You should be with Lockie."

I took two figs wrapped in gauze-thin prosciutto, thanked her and returned to the table where Lockie was explaining the intricacies of the electric gate.

"All because of your colt," I told Cam who was at the table with his parents, Kate and Fitch, as well as his grandfather, Kerwin.

Greer had vanished.

"It's Greer's colt and he is unusually gregarious. Try not being so uptight," Cam replied.

"We would just like the horses to stay where we put them," I replied.

"So regimented." Cam popped a wrapped fig in his mouth.

Kate smiled at me. "He's just teasing. Right, Cam? It's a party, let's all behave."

Fitch shook his head. "Least likely candidate of the three children to do so."

"Trouble from Day One," Kerwin said sotto voce.

"I'm only on the other side of the table. I can hear you, Gramps."

"Don't call me that."

"Boys." Kate tried to mediate.

It seemed to work.

By seven o'clock, everyone had arrived, Greer sat down with us, and Diego served the *Primi Piatti*, first course, which was one large eggplant mousse ravioli with a delicate butter and forest mushroom sauce. To everyone's credit, not one of the guests licked their plates.

Those plates were taken away and replaced with the *Secondi Piatti*. We had several choices and, at our table, we opted to make sure each was ordered by someone so we could all taste test. The *Osso Buco* was delicious and had been cooking slowly all day. Greer's *Pollo Fortunato* with roasted lemons was delectable.

By the time dessert arrived, I'd had enough, but Jules had made a deep chocolate cake with the silkiest of Italian buttercream frosting and there was no way I would pass that up. Diego had made an Italian rum cake and assorted fruit tarts, *crostata di frutta*.

"We have been well-fed," my father said, finishing his piece of cake. "Thank you for helping put this together, Jules."

"You're welcome. If Lockie is pleased, the many days of preparation were worth it," she said, teasingly.

"It was wonderful, Jules, but you never fail," Lockie replied.

"Gee, isn't that raising the bar to an impossible height?"

"Not at all," I assured her.

"And I?" Diego asked.

"Masterful," I said. "This restaurant will be a success and everyone will eat so much, you'll have to make the doors wider."

Everyone added their encouragement as they sipped their espresso or the various *aperitivi* Diego was passing around the table.

Lockie tasted his and offered it to me for a sip.

I took the smallest amount possible and nearly choked. "What is that?"

"*Gineprino*. It's made from juniper berries," Jules replied.

"Like from trees?"

"Yes."

"Are people crazy?" I asked.

Lockie kissed my cheek.

On their way out, the Becks and Hambletts stopped by the table to wish Lockie a happy birthday again and the girls handed him cards. Opening the envelope, he was doused with glitter that had fallen off the designs they made.

"Glitter is my favorite color," Poppy said with a grin.

"Shocker," Greer commented.

"See you tomorrow," I said and received hugs in return.

Lockie stood. "I think it's time for me to go home and Talia was my ride over, but you can stay, if you want."

"No, I'm ready to pack it in."

I kissed everyone, thanked them for coming, as Lockie did, and then we escaped into the damp night.

"I'm going out with the hounds tomorrow morning."

"I know. I hoped we could leave earlier."

"It's all right. Are you still coming out on Saturday?"

We got in the truck. "Yes, I promised Poppy she could ride Call. With the Hilltoppers. I don't think she's ready for the field."

"If she were in England, she would be."

"They don't have the same laws," I pointed out.

"What happened to assumed risk? I didn't sue anyone after my accident. It was an accident," Lockie said.

I wasn't entirely convinced of that. At some point, the event committee must take responsibility for the conditions horses and riders are competing under. I understood how everyone was keen to ride that day, even in the rain, but if the ground was too muddy, then the event might need to be halted. Who was to decide? Someone with more experience than I. Lockie thought it was safe, so perhaps he was right, that it was an accident.

"Talia," he started. "It was a good party. Thank you."

"It was, and you're welcome."

We arrived at home, one of the last times we'd be able to drive onto the property without waiting for the gate to open. Less than a half hour later, we were comfortably ready to go to sleep.

"I know you didn't want a present but—"

"Because you don't give a flip about what I say, you went ahead anyway," he replied.

"Yes. That's true." I handed him the box. "But I didn't wrap it."

"That's so much better."

Lockie opened the box and found the fountain pen. He held it in his hands, removed the cap, studied the nib and the stock pin clip then put it back in the box. After placing it on the nightstand, he turned off the light and pulled me close.

16

LOCKIE LEFT BEFORE FIRST LIGHT, putting Dice in his trailer and taking him to the Jamieson farm.

I sat in the kitchen, a cup of hot tea in front of me while Jules shaped the yeast dough that had been stored in the refrigerator since the previous morning.

"You must love cooking," I said to her.

"Why has it taken you over a year to notice?"

"Slow study. You cooked all of yesterday for Lockie's party and you're up at six making breakfast pastries."

"I could say the same about anyone here. When you find your passion, it's not work, it's—"

"An act of love," I finished for her.

"Exactly. We're here to serve. That's what gives meaning to our lives."

"That and ninety percent butterfat."

"Fat's where the flavor is." Jules laughed as she rolled out the dough.

Joly preceded Greer into the kitchen.

"Why is everyone up so early?" she asked.

"Lockie left over an hour ago, and I was the designated stable hand."

"You're crazy. Both of you. We were out late."

"I know but he's going to be their alternate Whip, so he can't tell Sibby it's too early when she was at the party with us and will be out there on her horse."

Greer yawned.

"When did you get home?" I asked.

"Midnight?" Greer asked Jules.

"I think so. We were the last table. The Coopers tell the most hilarious stories."

"Talking about Basta with Diego and show business gossip with the Coopers. Unbelievable. Madder than snakes, actors are."

Jules nodded in agreement as she began cutting the dough.

***

166

With Poppy on Calling All Comets, and Gincy on Beau, I schooled the Glitter Girls on the flat, then moved them to the outside course where we tried to prepare for the hunter pace later in the year. The course would be suitable for ponies and young riders so there would be some small fences they could jump. So far I was not convinced they could go together and without someone older, even if they insisted they could.

While their positions were good, what concerned me was that they hadn't had enough time in the saddle to instinctively close their legs as an emergency arose. I didn't want them to have a death grip on the saddle at all times, which would only produce tension in them and the ponies, but they had to learn to feel when they needed to be more secure. It was best if it was muscle memory and that took an investment of time. If Ami Gish had just gripped tighter when she felt Oneco's stumble coming, she might well have stayed on. But she didn't feel it and the Glitter Girls couldn't sense the need for greater contact when the need arose, either.

Poppy wanted to move up to the next level, but this inability was what kept her where she was. They could both get away with a certain degree of looseness on the flat and over small fences in the ring, the hunt field was too unpredictable. The terrain was uneven, there were large horses, hounds and riders who shouldn't be there, either.

I needed to see both girls stick to the saddle no matter what happened. Then I would be convinced they were ready to be faced with greater challenges, not before.

Ami Gish might not have learned anything from me, but I learned a great deal from her. I wasn't going to see one of my riders sailing through the air and landing on the fence because I hadn't drilled them hard enough.

"I want you to jump the low fences, and remain in your two-point position. I don't want to see pump and bump," I said.

Was there something I could paint on the saddle that would prove to them they were falling back into the seat? One of those soap crayons in a bright color? I'd have to do a search on the Internet.

The two girls went around the field, Poppy at a hand gallop on Call and Gincy on a more reserved canter with Beau. That Gincy was thinking was appealing to me. That Poppy was bold was also appealing. I tried to assess their performances without my own bias showing, but didn't succeed. Lockie was the template. He thought and was confident. To be both in equal amounts was rare. I wasn't even sure if his qualities were in balance, but certainly more than any other rider I had known.

Me? I thought too much.

Cam was bold.

Greer had always been impatient to see results. Now, she had taken a sabbatical even if she didn't call it that. For the first time in her life, she had started to ride for pleasure.

"Lockie's back!" Gincy announced as his truck and trailer came down the drive.

"Can we go talk to him? He can tell us about the hunt!" Poppy said.

"I didn't realize we were finished here," I replied.

"Sorry."

"One more time. I want your knees flat on the saddle, not turned away. That pulls your entire leg out of position." I pressed Poppy's knee against the flap and rearranged her lower leg. "The longer you ride, the more attention you will pay to small details."

Gincy smiled.

She liked details and I was so pleased at the progress Gincy had made over the last few months. She wasn't the same rider who had come to me last year.

Poppy was the same. She wanted to go fast, and jump higher. The specifics didn't interest her as much as the adrenaline rush, but to her credit, Poppy always tried.

They rode the course again, the effort apparent.

"Okay. Good job. You can go talk to Lockie."

"Yay."

They cantered away from me as he and Cap were taking Dice out of the trailer. By the time I reached the yard, they were grilling him mercilessly about the morning's outing.

Poppy wanted to know how big the jumps were and Gincy wanted to know about the puppies. How small were they?

"They're not eight weeks old. They're teenage dogs," Lockie explained.

He told them about the kennels and the kennelman or huntsman, depending on the hunt. The girls listened with rapt attention.

I wasn't sure if it was Lockie they were interested in or the hunt or a combination. They did adore him, understandably.

Lockie answered all their questions as Cap took Dice into the barn to clean up and return to his stall for the midday shift. Later, he would go out to pasture with his friends, CB and Henry.

"Go take care of your ponies," I said before they had a chance to start in on a new round of questions.

"They'll pass inspection with flying colors!" Poppy assured me as they went off to the lower barn.

Lockie kissed me. "They're so excited to see me. Why aren't you?"

"I am, I just hide it better."

"I can't be a rock star to everyone." He walked to the cab of the truck and opened the door. "Day gave me a present."

Lockie removed a large rectangular package from the cab.

"Surprise."

"I'm so sure. You've been planning these things for months."

"Yes." I laughed. "I didn't want to get you something from the Dollarama."

"Should I open it here or should there be a ceremony and background music?"

"Just open it. I'll show it to everyone else later."

The moment he pulled the paper back, the image took my breath. Day had painted Lockie on Dice in the hunt field surrounded by hounds, just looking out over the hills. There was a sense of quietude that lifted off the canvas and enveloped me. She had captured his essence, somehow, in the line of his back, the focus of his gaze, the way he holds the reins.

I put my forehead against his chest.

"What, Silly?"

"It's perfectly you."

"There's a likeness," he admitted.

"Yesterday, I didn't say all the things I wanted to say but I knew you didn't want to hear them."

"They're just words. Thoughts are what you do each day. That counts."

"I—"

An expensive SUV pulled up in front of the barn, stopped and Victoria got out. She was still in her breeches and boots from the cubbing.

"Hi. What's that?"

Lockie turned the painting around. "It's a birthday present."

Victoria studied the image, critically. "I'll have to get Day some commission work. She's too good not to use that talent."

"What can I do for you, Victoria?" Lockie asked.

"I want to know what the status of our trial trade is."

"I thought we were looking at a month."

"I don't need a month."

"Do you want me to bring Dice back this afternoon?"

"I don't want him. I want Kyff," Victoria said.

Lockie paused. "He's Tali's project, so it would be her decision."

Victoria turned to me, questioningly.

"What do you want to do with him?" I asked.

"Hunt, of course, and there's the Newbury Hounds show next month. Does that seem odd to you?"

I thought for a moment. "Yes."

"It shouldn't. Horseback riding was my first sport. Tennis was much later but I don't find that galumping around after a ball speaks to my true nature."

"I believe that," I replied.

"Good. So Kyff and I get along and unlike, God knows, my past which has been anything but predictable except for its unpredictability, it would be good to know you won't be asking for him back while I'm in the middle of making plans."

I quickly came up with several scenarios where he might be needed at home.

"Don't be a horse hoarder," Lockie said to me.

"I won't take him to England without permission, is that better for you?" Victoria asked.

"He was mistreated in his former life and I want the best for him. I like him," I replied.

"I like him, too," Victoria said, "and I'd like to take some dressage lessons on him, if you can tolerate us, Lockie. Greg is very good with the jumping but has confessed he knows very little about dressage."

"Are you going to ride sidesaddle, too?"

"I might. Greer's, not surprisingly, excellent at it. She's one of those people who can do anything she puts her mind to."

"So are you," I countered.

"I..." Victoria shrugged. "Is Andrew home?"

"Yes, he's up at the house. Why don't you stay for lunch?"

"Thank you for inviting me. That's the whole point of visiting at lunchtime, isn't it?" Victoria gave us a little wave, got in her SUV and drove up to the house.

"There's something I've been wondering about," I said.

"Ask."

"Historically, you've ridden complicated, high energy horses. Wing is a Thoroughbred. The Acadiana horses are forward and sensitive."

"It's always a fascinating journey to travel with you to the point you're trying to make."

I nodded. "Creatively, what do you get out of Dice?"

"Creatively?"

It seemed like the wrong word choice. I tried again. "What's the challenge?"

"Because he's in a good mood all the time, and doesn't have a swish or go sideways?"

"Those attributes, right."

"I'm not a cowboy."

"Intellectually—"

Lockie smiled. "There are riders who want the horse to be different every day. I ride a number of different horses a day, all with their own personalities, quirks and temperaments. What you may be seeing as a liability, I'm seeing as an asset. I don't have to retrain him, coddle him or cajole him. Dice just wants to do the job. That simplifies my life."

"Is he enough for you?"

"Yes, plenty. I enjoy riding him. Everything's okay, Tal."

"Except I'm being sued and you were arrested for assault."

"Nothing little things. Let's go have lunch. The ladies are coming for their one o'clock."

***

After watching the lesson with the ami-owners, I thought they were good riders and the horses were cute. Their equestrian educations had some large holes revealed by Lockie when he asked them to do a few exercises, a gymnastic and to perform the simple task of a half halt.

Standing in the center of the ring, we all talked about what they felt was good and what was lacking in their training.

"We don't aspire to win ribbons," Joan started.

"It's always nice," Sandy said.

"We want to be better riders and have more fun with our horses. I may be a mother but there's still a pony-mad kid in me."

"I understand," I said.

"If you don't have an expensive horse and a great deal of money, some stables won't take you seriously," Sandy added. "This is like going back to college for me. I want to pick up where I left off and learn for the enjoyment of it, not make it a career or get my picture in *On The Rail Magazine*."

"That would be nice, though," Joan admitted. "The ladies at the garden club would be very impressed between discussions about eradicating poison ivy and the new yellow geranium."

"Unlike other sports," Lockie started, "there isn't such a pressing need to be young. The oldest equestrian who competed in the Olympic Games was seventy-one. You can

175

continue to grow and learn and improve for your entire life. To live is to learn."

"We're also taught by our horses," I said.

"Take Talia's horse for example," Lockie added. "He keeps trying to teach me to stay out of his saddle but I just keep going back for more."

The women laughed as we left the arena.

Lockie liked to end each session on a positive note and he had done so again. I had so much to learn from him about teaching and each class was like a seminar for me.

Cap came out of the barn with her horse, Bijou. "I'm your tour guide for the next hour," she said to the women. "I'll show you some of the trails and familiarize you with the area. We've never had to send out a search team yet, so we're counting on you not to be the first."

"I have GPS on my phone," Sandy replied.

"That should help where we have service." Cap mounted. "Oh, Lockie. A British guy called. He's looking for a horse and someone suggested you. I left the phone number on the white board."

"Can you be a little more specific? A name perhaps?"

"Tarrant Heath," Cap replied and started up the driveway.

"Where have I heard that name before?" Lockie asked me.

"He's Mark Kobayashi's new trainer and Greer's ex-boyfriend."

"You're not serious."

"Yes, he's at the old Far Reach Farm."

"Talia. You know I meant Greer."

"I was trying to avoid that part."

"Please tell me they ended on good terms."

I was silent.

"That bad?"

"It probably made The Boer War look like a weekend in Majorca," I said. "He's from a more aristocratic family than the Rowes. He never stopped lording it over her."

"What does that mean? His ancestors had fewer qualms about drawing and quartering their enemies?"

"That's how one climbed the ladder of nobility," I replied.

"We have to keep Greer away from him."

❧ 17 ❧

"THAT'S A GIVEN," I replied.

Greer meeting up with Tarrant Heath again was not a scenario I wanted to see.

"I'll call him and find out what Lord Heathcliff wants."

Lockie disappeared into the barn. I got into my truck and drove to the house where Victoria was kissing my father goodbye.

"About Dice and Kyff," I started.

My father turned to the house. "I don't want to hear about horses. Have a good afternoon, Victoria."

"You, too," she replied. "I recognize the look on your face. It's the Swope Lets-Make-A-Deal expression."

"Let's take a walk."

"Complicated deal," Victoria replied as we headed for the flower garden Parti had not yet trampled into the dirt.

"Your former neighbor is probably coming here this afternoon."

"What neighbor would that be?"

"Tarrant Heath."

She nodded. "From back home."

"And I want to make sure Greer and he don't happen to run into each other."

"It's impossible to avoid all the people who have insulted you or that you have insulted. I know this from experience."

"Greer doesn't need to be re-upset. She's doing pretty well right now and I want to keep it that way."

"What do you suggest?"

"You can have custody of Kyff..."

"Until?"

"I don't know. Let's solve one issue at a time. Keep him, hunt him, show him, be nice to him and we can work out the details later. This afternoon and any time in the future where Princeling Heath is concerned, you get Greer out of the way."

"How am I supposed to do that?" Victoria asked logically.

"Tell her you want her input about the Thoroughbreds Greg rescued. Take her to Rowe House Farm and let her inspect them."

"Are they gaining weight, bright-eyed and bushy-tailed, that sort of thing?"

"Yes."

"Tell her I have the pony riders this afternoon and can't go with you. Tell her you think one of them may have an ulcer and you want her opinion."

"Why wouldn't I just call the vet?"

"Geez, Victoria, as though you can't tell a story."

"She hates me."

"You hurt her feelings. This will make up for it, if you try hard enough. Try acting like..." I stopped.

"Sarah?"

"I'm not trying to insult you. Make friends with her. She can be a porcupine but you can do it."

"It runs in the family," Victoria said as we paused by a Butterfly Bush.

"What does?"

"Difficult relationships. I disappointed my mother. Marrying Andrew?" She brushed her hand across the purple blossoms. "My mother never forgave me for that and never forgave me for letting him go." She smiled. "I'd write about it but I don't want fame to detract from her nobility."

I smiled.

"See. You were amused."

"Be like this with Greer and you'll see her start to come around."

Victoria shrugged. "How long do I have to keep her at Rowe House, because he's not here yet?"

"I'll call."

Victoria turned and walked toward the house. "It's a plan. I wouldn't assess it as brilliant..."

I jogged down the hill to the barn and ran inside thinking at least there was a plan.

"Where did you go?"

"To have Greer kidnapped so she doesn't run into Heathcliff Manor."

"Is Cam here?"

"No, Victoria."

"At least it's a plan," Lockie admitted.

I realized no one was going to be excited by my solution but at least they were willing to go along with it. "Is Tarrant coming here?"

"Yes, he's in Pawling so it'll be an hour or so."

Poppy, Gincy and Annie ran into the barn.

"I have the pony riders," I said, as they greeted us enthusiastically.

"I can ride!" Annie assured me. "I just can't do anything that will shake me up too much."

Of course they had to start shaking and bouncing on the aisle.

"Enough. I get it. Annie, I know you're not going to the cubbing with us so you can ride your pony. Poppy will ride Beau and Gincy will ride Knock Knock. We're not going to ask too much of him, but we'll make you all ride without stirrups to compensate."

They protested mightily.

"Just for that, take the stirrups off the saddles, you won't need them at all."

"But Talia, no one has ridden Knock Knock. What if he bucks me off?"

"Greer rode him and said he's a very well-mannered gentleman. If he bucks you off what does that tell us?"

"That my legs weren't tight enough on the saddle."

"Correct. What's the remedy for that?"

"Riding without stirrups," Gincy replied.

"Go get your ponies."

They ran out and headed for the lower barn.

Lockie nuzzled against my neck. "You're so good with them it makes me wish I was short enough to ride ponies. If I had a teacher like you when I was nine, I would have had a permanent grin on my face that would have made people ask if I was from Stupidtown."

Picturing him as a small boy, trotting around the ring with a smile from ear to ear made me laugh. I wished I had been there. Of course, I would have been about three and had not yet expressed an interest in horses or boys.

He put his arms around me. "If you can't teach me how to ride will you spot me on Tsai?"

"If you're riding for twenty minutes, ride in with the ponies and you can demonstrate to them."

"Then can we have a jump school before Heathbar shows up?"

"You can demonstrate that, too."

"Since when do I have to cut deals with you?"

"Today's a deal day," I replied.

"It's the Swope side of the family. Brutal." Lockie walked away shaking his head.

Ten minutes later the Glitter Girls were shocked into silence by Lockie joining their lesson. As he crossed his irons in front of the saddle, they whispered between each other, not knowing he routinely rode without stirrups. Whether he had them or not made no difference. He had a beautifully correct position no matter what he did. Whether in the hunt field or show jumping, it was elegant and balanced. The number of hours in the saddle that made that possible was substantial but still less than the dedication required to achieve such control.

"Whether you have your stirrups or not, your leg should be in position. Heels down, toes pointed forward. If you allow your toe to turn too much away from straight ahead, the lower leg will pull away from the horse's sides. You want the inside of your leg flat against the horse."

Annie was struggling with this more than Gincy and Poppy.

"If you were wearing spurs, as I am," Lockie added, "and I allowed my leg to turn away from the horse as Talia is describing, look what happens."

183

The pony riders watched as Lockie jogged in front of them.

"The spur is poking the horse's side," Gincy said.

"Besides being unkind, what happens?" I asked.

"The horse responds to an aid you're not giving on purpose," Poppy answered.

"That's right. Good girl," I said. "When we ride, we are trying to communicate with someone who doesn't understand our language. We have to be as clear with our requests as possible. Trot on."

Cap and I moved around the poles for the pony-size gymnastic.

"Let's see if we can get around the ring twice in your half-seat position while trotting," I called to them. "Grab mane if you need some help with your balance but don't rely on it. Use your legs."

Annie was having the hardest time.

With Lockie, there was no difference between when he had stirrups and when he didn't.

"The stirrup is supposed to be a rest for your foot. Not a floor that you're standing on. It's an aid to be used but not overused."

"That doesn't sound right to me," Poppy said.

"I once saw a rider have a stirrup leather come right off the saddle in an open jumping class. He finished the round without it and placed."

"Really?" Gincy asked, sitting down and pulling back into a sitting trot.

Lockie trotted past and gave me a look.

"Yes. It was very exciting," I replied. "What if he relied heavily on having two stirrups? That would have been the end of the competition for him."

Poppy nodded.

"Walk, please. Thinking of how it feels to have stirrups, try to reproduce that same feeling without. Don't pinch your knees onto the saddle in a death grip now when you don't do it regularly. Part of the secret is balance. Learn how to find your balance without the foot rest. You will need less effort if your body is in alignment. Is that true, Lockie?"

"Very true. Balance on your thighs."

I had them canter.

Lockie was beautiful in the saddle, of course. It was rare to see a man ride as precisely and gracefully as he did. To see him work was to know that was how it was supposed to be done. While I thought he had been blessed with the ideal body type, long leg from hip to knee and long arms, Lockie insisted he was too long in the back. I didn't see it.

Tsai was a gorgeous Acadiana horse we had been working with while Teche was taking time off back home in Louisiana. He was a little temperamental, a little demanding and quick to react to anything that happened. Not my kind of horse. Cee was the perfect fit for me. He brought out the best in me and I managed to stay on.

Before my pony riders were completely worn out, I had them trot over the gymnastic. It was just some poles on the ground, but the extra clearance the horses gave was enough to give Annie some trouble.

Lockie spent the time doing leg yields at the other end of the ring and Gincy's attention was focused on him.

Cap and I reconfigured the gymnastic for Tsai's benefit and Lockie came over to me.

"You can pick up your stirrups if you want," I said.

"No, it'll be good for them to see into their future if they keep going."

To be serious about riding meant work every day, very little time off. It meant being coached forever. It meant wearing your breeches out, your boots, your gloves. It meant being dirty, sweaty, tired and hungry most of the time.

It also meant being privileged to have relationships with great personalities, both horses and some people.

"Tsai hasn't been as steady and predictable as Lockie would like," I said to the girls. "We've set up this gymnastic to get Tsai to concentrate on what's in front of him, not so much on what's around him."

At a show, Tsai was bothered by the public address system, golf carts, small dogs on leashes, baby carriages, and tents flapping in the breeze. He was talented and eye-catching, but behaved like a kid with ADHD. Everything distracted him.

To the right rider, these might not be huge problems, but the average rider would find Tsai difficult. We didn't want to send horses into the world who could be expected to have trouble adjusting to real life.

In our program, he had been given lots of flat work, gymnastics, trail riding and pasture time. Progress was slow but Tsai's outlook was improving.

It was Lockie's goal to have any of our horses able to be ridden well by a relatively accomplished amateur. That meant, to a degree, they had to be bomb-proof. The horses who didn't have that disposition were likely to be found homes where professionals would handle them.

"What are his special talents?" Gincy asked.

"He had potential as a show jumper," I replied. "You can take a walk in the woods, and I mean walk. Cross the stream, loop around and come back by the road."

That would take them about a half hour. If they were gone much longer, I would send out a search party. It was good for them to develop confidence and independence, but not too much at once.

Lockie worked Tsai over the small course he had created earlier in the day. It was a change from what he had done before and presented a slight challenge but by the end of the ride, Tsai settled down and relaxed.

"Will you ride him next week, Tal?" Lockie asked as he slid off.

"I think you're better off with Greer. She likes hot horses."

"Which is why her main squeeze is Tea Biscuit instead of Citabria."

"So either you or Cam start showing Bria."

"Talk her into leasing them." Lockie ran up his stirrups.

An expensive foreign car came down the drive and parked near us. As the two men got out, I quickly texted Victoria to keep Greer there until I gave the all clear.

"Hi."

It had to be Tarrant because he had the accent.

"Lockie. I'm Tarrant Heath. I think we met at Bromley some years back."

Lockie nodded and held out his hand for the shake.

I wasn't sure by his expression whether he remembered or not. Lockie had met a lot of people in the horse world and no one could remember all of them.

"This is Mark Kobayashi, the owner of the barn."

I shook his hand.

"What are you looking for?"

"A show jumper with potential," Tarrant said. "Is this gelding for sale?"

"He could be but he's not a Bittersweet horse. He's probably not as far along as you'd like. You want to go to Florida for the winter?"

188

"Yes," Tarrant replied.

"I wouldn't take him but we do things in slow motion compared to everyone else."

"That's what I was told," Mark said to Lockie.

"There's our reputation preceding us," I commented.

"Where's Greer?" Tarrant asked.

"Out for the afternoon," I replied.

Cap took Tsai from Lockie.

Lockie began to walk toward the lower barn. "Let me take you on a tour. I have some Acadiana horses here, and a couple of our own. Maybe you'll see something that interests you."

"I saw Cam Rafferty ride a horse called Counterpoint earlier in the year," Mark started. "Is that horse for sale?"

We reached the barn. "Technically, he's not a Bittersweet horse, he's Greer Swope's horse," Lockie replied.

"I can talk to her." Tarrant exuded confidence, and why not, he was extremely handsome for anyone who wasn't a fashion model. He was a British aristocrat and socially well-connected. "We go way back."

If I were him, I'd be watching my back.

He'd be lucky if she didn't run him down and back over him a couple times with the van.

After an hour, the two horses they were most interested in were Debandade and Kid Gaucho, a horse Cam had gotten from someone in Arizona who thought the market was better out East than where he was. Lockie had ridden

189

them, then Tarrant had gotten on to take them over a few fences.

I thought Tarrant was what I expected of a minor level show jumper. He was okay. He knew what he had to do to get around a course. His position was not an element that concerned him particularly but that wasn't unusual. There was no equitation division in England for riders to go through the way Lockie had. If they hadn't been exposed to eventing with a good dose of dressage, then hanging on and expecting good results was a plan.

Mark Kobayashi seemed to be willing to invest money in acquiring a string of show jumpers and the farm in Westchester had to have cost millions of dollars. With Tarrant, he had gotten a young professional who had not proven himself or disproven himself yet. Sometimes an unknown quantity was the root of appeal.

Leaving Lockie to talk to the two men, I went inside to text Victoria that she should give it another half hour and then Heathcliff would be gone. I wondered if we'd have to go through this again to prevent an upset.

Ten minutes later Mark and Tarrant got into the expensive foreign car and left. Two minutes later, Greer came flying into the barn.

"Tell me I didn't see what I just saw!"

"Give us a hint," Cap said.

"Tarrant Heath."

"How did you see him through the tinted windows," Lockie asked.

I glared at him. "You didn't have to admit it so fast."

"It's not a secret, she knows."

"It was him? What was he doing here?"

"Looking at horses." Lockie put Dice on the aisle.

"This is not acceptable!"

"Just because you have a history with him—"

"What nonsensical thing are you going to say?"

"Not a thing," Cap replied and went to the feed room.

"My mother was in on this," Greer said, then looked at me. "You were in on it!"

"Yes, we were all in on it. It was a huge conspiracy to save you from having this implosion."

"You so do not understand!" Greer strode out of the barn.

"That went better than I thought it would," Lockie said.

⟡ 18 ⟡

EARLY THE NEXT MORNING we went to Jamieson Farm for the cub hunt. Again, it was like a caravan. Lockie didn't have to tell me that we could get one huge trailer and solve all our problems, but I was disinclined to change what we had. I liked the van. Even if it was old, it had style. It was painted in our stable colors and Pavel insisted it would last forever with the amount of use we gave it.

Cam had taken the Acadiana horses Tropiezienne, Skandal, and a couple others up to Canada for a huge show, so he wasn't around for something as modest as a cub hunt. He kept the farm running for Teche, placing often, winning sometimes. I was glad he had been able to be in town for

Lockie's birthday party but I had become very fond of him and when he was on the road, I did miss him.

We made sure Lockie got on Dice early because he was staff, then we helped the pony riders and made sure everything was right for them. Excited to be participating in their first hunt, Joan and Sandy managed on their own with some input from Cap.

Greer stopped me in the van as I was getting ready to take CB down the ramp.

"You don't understand about Tarrant."

"Do you want to explain it?"

"No," Greer replied. "He's not a nice person. He gets away with it because of his looks and his family's prestige."

"All right. I won't ask any questions. You can tell me when you're ready. What would you like us to do?"

Greer unclipped Tea. "Don't have anything to do with him. We don't need him."

"Okay, I will tell Lockie."

"I'll owe you."

"No, you won't. It's family."

"Will Lockie see it that way and not business?"

"Yes, he will."

Tea followed Greer out of the van and then I got CB on the ground. Cap held Tea while Greer donned her sidesaddle habit, then helped her into the saddle. To say Greer looked stunning was minimizing how beautiful she was and I wished she could see herself as I saw her.

She looked down at me with a smile so delicate that it could have broken apart with a sudden puff of air.

There was a photographer from the local paper shooting everything that the readers might find interesting. Poppy and Gincy posed for her. Lockie didn't bother to stand still while trying to get the puppies to pack in. Greer adjusted her veil and that was another shot.

Then Sibby led us into the field.

***

Waiting for us back at the farm, Jules had prepared a hunt breakfast of grits and cheese, scrambled eggs, chicken sausage patties, fresh rolls, and fruit salad with mint. There was iced tea, iced coffee, sparkling peach juice, frittatas and Diego, who charmed everyone as he served or pushed more food at the guests.

The rain that had held off for the entire meet began and I hoped Lockie would finish his conversation with Sibby and get home. I never liked the thought of a horse trailer being hauled over wet roads.

As the last of the guests left, Lockie's rig pulled down the driveway. I excused myself and went to help him with Dice.

They were in the wash stall when I arrived. Dice looked the same as when he left and was happy for the cookie I offered him. The peppermint variety was his favorite flavor.

"That was a long talk you had with Sibby."

"She didn't want to talk," Lockie said, holding the spray of water on Dice's legs. "One of the members couldn't see herself home so Victoria and I took care of it."

"Gee, what happened to her?"

"Her flask happened to her," Lockie replied.

That wasn't good. "What's her name?"

Lockie thought. "Mrs. Krummelkucken."

I paused. "Is that her real name?"

"I don't remember her real name. Something that's like the word for crumb cake."

I laughed. "I'm sorry. I couldn't help it."

"Well, neither could she, apparently." He turned off the water. "Sibby did have a talk with me to change my status."

"Not an alternate anymore?" I asked.

"No. Joint."

"Oh, good for you! Are you pleased?"

He put his arms around me. "It's a responsibility."

"What's your concern?"

"Scheduling."

I gave him a squeeze. "It's only for part of the year."

"When I was eight or so, there was an earthquake in the area where we lived. It seemed to last for about ten minutes but it was less than a minute. The ground rolled under my feet like standing on a waterbed. It lost its integrity. Everything in the world was shifting."

"I understand."

"I'm saying this because you do."

I kissed him. "Let's put Dice in his stall. Then you can go up to the house for lunch and Diego can tell you all about his revised menu at Basta."

"He's here?"

"A normal meal becomes a party when he's around. Doesn't he ever get tired?" I wondered.

"No."

After walking Dice to his stall, I gave him an apple cookie, which he took happily because that was his favorite flavor. We got into my truck and drove up to the house in the rain.

I wished the weather put the rest of the day's work aside, but that was impossible. There were always horses to be ridden, chores to be done. We could have a lunch hour, even though I couldn't eat another thing until dinner.

Greer was studying her phone. "Waiting for the results of the hunter derby up at Pigeonnet Farm."

Lockie went into the house to wash his hands and Jules brought him a sandwich layered with chicken, roasted red peppers and flowingly soft St. Andre cheese.

"I don't know why we can't have streaming video of it," Greer commented.

I sat across from her. "How many horses were in the class?"

"Fifty something."

"A derby?" Diego asked and mimicked putting on a hat.

"Not that kind of derby," I said. "It's a competition over jumps for money."

Diego nodded. "Money, I understand. The horses, no. I can learn. All things American!"

"Except the food," Greer pointed out.

"Not at Basta." Diego thought. "Hot dog pizza?"

"NO!"

"With that cabbage...what's it called?"

"Sauerkraut."

"Wet," he said.

I nodded.

Diego's mind was working. If he could make a spaghetti and meatball sandwich, I was sure he could make a hot dog and sauerkraut pizza.

He and Jules were so creative. Sassy Collins was always inventing some dog treat. Greer designed her sidesaddle habits. I had no skills.

I could back the trailer up without hitting anything. That was something to take pride in.

"Yes!" Greer cheered. "Cam won the derby!"

"Fantastic! Is there a photo?"

"No, just the results."

"We could call to congratulate him—"

"—if he had a phone," Greer finished my thought.

"Call him tonight at the motel."

"I don't know where he's staying," Greer replied.

"Call Acadiana and ask," I suggested.

"I wouldn't do that."

"Maybe it would make him feel good," I said. "Like if you were thinking about him for a minute or so."

"You could call him and make him feel—"

"Forget I mentioned it," I said and went into the house.

***

At eight the next morning, we took the caravan to the state park to ride the main trail, which took about an hour. By the time we had finished the loop, people had started to arrive for their picnics and volleyball games. It was time for us to leave.

The weather report was for high temperatures and uncomfortable humidity due to the rain we'd had the day before. Lockie wanted to get the riding out of the way early and let everyone have the rest of day off.

Poppy was going to the beach. Gincy was off to a friend's house where they had a pool. Joan and Sandy were going to spend time with their families and do things like weed the garden.

Greer, Jules and I went to the 4-H Fair to check on the progress being made. The girls were happy, picking up a few ribbons. One of them, deservedly, got the blue in Fitting and Showing, but for others the braids had been rubbed loose overnight and tails hadn't been braided at all.

It was the biggest show of the year for most of them and many were very rough around the edges. Greer and I wondered how we could help polish them up in the most cost effective manner. Having clothes that fit would be an excellent beginning and we decided that finding a source of good used show gear was on our to-do list. We wondered if a morning where we could just teach them the finer points of preparation would be welcomed.

Not all the girls in the 4-H club rode with me and I didn't want to imply other teachers weren't giving them the best information.

I didn't have the best of reputations in the county at the moment anyway so was reluctant to say anything.

Jules bought several crocheted dishcloths and a jar of jelly from the handcrafts tent which pleased the young sellers, then we returned to the farm.

There was business for Lockie to catch up on and I knew he was tired, so I did my barn chores then spent a few hours reading while doing the laundry. I planned to take CB out in the evening for a hack, the way I had done with Butch. I liked having that time with him, just the two of us. Instead, Victoria called and invited us to her farm for a stylish summer weekend in the country dinner that I thought was research for one of her books.

We returned home too late to ride but had to wait for Parti to get off the driveway so we could get to the house.

Lockie was tired and fell asleep almost immediately. I read for a while, then gave up. After midnight, Cam finally called to say they had made it back to the farm, later than planned because the truck had broken down in Upstate New York. I knew Greer had been worried about him on the long drive but she could have called the barn manager at Acadiana. Good idea except that then someone would suspect she had feelings for him. That was something she didn't want anyone to know.

***

Mondays were supposed to be our day off but that just meant we caught up on everything else we didn't do for the rest of the week.

Tea had a loose shoe, Knock needed to be shod, Butch and the ponies needed to be trimmed so the farrier was on the aisle all morning. Lockie was on the phone all morning, taking calls about horses or making calls about them. I didn't think we needed any more horses but I was wrong because Cam brought us a dark bay, seventeen-two hand gelding from Canada named Indicus.

I stood by the fence and watched this horse trot around the paddock. He looked hot. He looked like he didn't fit in here.

Greer came up to me. "Who's supposed to handle him?"

"Good question. We need to keep the girls away from him."

The horse snorted and whirled.

"Maybe Cam has a buyer for him."

"We have an appointment, so can you just get in the truck and leave now or do you have to change?"

Greer, of course, looked perfect.

"I'm relatively clean. Where are we going?"

"Mrs. Meade set up a go-see with the head of the 4-H, a Mrs. Noonan. I have all the notes on setting up a non-riding seminar we can hold at the ring at Selby Park."

I don't know why I was surprised. "When did you do this?"

"We talked about it yesterday."

"I don't remember talking about a seminar."

"We talked about doing something."

I nodded. There was no point in arguing with Greer about it. It was going to happen and I just had to get on board before I got dragged along on my stomach.

She started to get in her truck.

"Why don't we take my truck? It has air."

"I have air."

"You mean roll down the windows kind of air conditioning?"

"Yes." She sat down and closed the door.

I gave in and sat in the passenger seat. A moment later we were going up the driveway, turned toward town and passed the construction crew who were going to install our gate.

This truck had been our birthday present to her last year, but it had been Cam's project. Most of the time it was parked in the garage. Then, without giving me a reason, she'd drive it. I thought it was a weather vane of sorts. She drove it when the emotional winds shifted for her about Cam.

"Everything's in the folder. Read it so you're familiar with what we want to do."

We, I thought as I opened up the presentation, I hadn't even been consulted.

Not surprisingly, in just a few easy to understand pages, Greer explained the goal of the seminar completely. It sounded so informative, I would have wanted to attend if I hadn't been roped into being one of the presenters.

Greer had already called Dr. Denise Newbold, the veterinarian in town and asked if she would like to give a lecture on horse health, provided she had time. Denise was more than happy to do so.

Cap had been enlisted to talk about basic horse care.

Sassy Collins at Eat Dog Eat, the shop uptown that sold gourmet dog meals, had agreed to make small packages of horse treats to give to each participant.

My talk was on equipment.

I felt stiffed.

Equipment? Who wants to listen to a talk about the width of stirrup leathers?

"Are you serious, Greer? Equipment?"

"Are you complaining?"

"You could have given me something a little more exciting."

"That's right. Proper fitting bits and saddles is one of the least important considerations a trainer has."

"I'm not saying that's not important but how much can you say about it to young girls who probably can't afford a new saddle."

"You don't want to do it, I'll do it."

"What were you going to do?"

"Braiding," Greer replied.

Greer was as good at braiding as any top groom on the circuit.

I didn't reply.

"Do you want to do both modules together?"

I reached over and touched her hand on the gear shift. "That would be wonderful."

She drove into the parking lot of the County Extension Service and parked in front of the building. "Then that's what we'll do."

19

"THE WOMAN from the newspaper called," Cap said when Greer and I returned from our hack with the pony riders.

"About?" I asked.

"She heard about the seminar and wants to come here for a visit to talk about that." Cap put jumping boots on Jetzt who was going out for a session with Cam and Lockie. "Also, she heard about riding sidesaddle on the hunt and thinks that's awfully interesting."

Greer brought Bria to the wash stall. "Did you get her number?" She called back, then turned on the water, guaranteeing the answer could not be heard.

"I left it in her office," Cap said. "Do you girls need any help?"

"Can we do it alone and then you can check our work?" Poppy asked.

"Sure."

Poppy, Gincy and Annie led their ponies to the lower barn, trying to remind themselves of everything they had to do. Cap didn't let them get away with anything and they knew it.

"Is Greer the first person in seventy-five years to ride sidesaddle on the hunt?" Cap asked as she adjusted Jetzt's noseband.

"Probably." I put Obilot on the crossties.

"That's newsworthy," Cap said.

I wasn't sure we could take more news about our lives. The man at the feed store had heard from the shavings guy who heard from someone over in Reynold's Bridge that I had something to do with a child falling off a pony. I told him she wasn't my student when it happened, paid for the feed and left.

It was so unfortunate I was getting the publicity instead of Paul Gish because as an actor he would court publicity good or bad as long as his name was spelled correctly.

I vowed never to work with another actor.

Cam came into the barn. "Hi, Tal. Want to ride Indicus for me today?"

"He's not my kind of horse," I replied, "although he has settled down a little on the ground."

It was difficult having a horse who required rules. We had children and amateurs who weren't familiar with a high performance horse and they could get into trouble.

"He's really more of a show-off than lit up."

"It takes a certain kind of disposition to appreciate that temperament in a horse. You think it's fun."

"I do, but I understand your concerns. He'll be gone soon."

"Where's Greer?" Cam asked.

"In the wash stall."

Cam unclipped Jetzt and walked him outside.

Cap looked at me and shrugged.

There was nothing I could say.

After taking care of Obilot, I headed to the indoor to see what was left of Cam's training session. Instantly I was aware of the different tenor. These were two professionals at work. Not an instructor and student. Equals. Cam and Lockie had experiences and knew techniques I would never know or need to know.

It made me feel as though I was unprepared to teach. Maybe I was partially responsible for Ami's accident. Maybe I could have worked with her more. Did I fail her?

Lockie's background was so extensive. He had ridden with the top teachers in the country, he had worked in

Ireland, studied in Germany, then ridden with Dan Ruhlmann who was a top eventer.

We had a series of incompetents making a half-hearted effort to teach us something. Most of our lessons were about the perfection of position and counting strides between fences. We didn't know anything about dressage, jumpers or even the hunter division.

Rui and several of our other coaches defrauded my family. They stole from us. Time that could have been used productively had been wasted. That could never be gotten back.

How did this happen? How were we all so taken advantage of by these people?

We had a nice farm and enough money to look very comfortable. Greer was a bitch and the other sister was sour. Why care?

Not one of us knew what was needed. I was mourning the loss of my mother and Greer was desperate to be good enough. The Swope business had hit a downturn and my father did everything he knew how to save it. He couldn't have wanted to be the Swope who lost the jewel he had inherited after so much work had gone into creating it.

He thought he was doing the right thing for us. Every trainer came to us with a good reputation. Every one of them had produced winning riders. Not one of them had taken the time to know us.

Not until Lockie.

Someone who had so little, who had lost so much, had rescued us.

I walked across the ring to him and kissed his cheek. "You're my favorite person," I said.

"You're my favorite person," he said.

Watching us, Cam let the reins drop on Jetzt's neck and held up his hands questioningly.

"I'll bring you two a couple smoothies. What flavor would you like?" I offered.

***

When I saw Greer wearing her sidesaddle habit, there was nothing to do but pity her. The afternoon temperatures were in the nineties and she was wearing a heavy long skirt, jacket and topper. Of course, she looked stunning. It was her newly designed dark purple outfit, cording down the front and at the sleeves, with a white ruffled stock tie.

We had decided to hold the interview in the house where it was slightly cooler, then go outside for the photography. Cap would have Tea ready so there would be no delay. Then the reporter would leave and Greer could change as quickly as possible. I did have concerns that she would faint if she stood in the sun for a protracted amount of time.

Down at the barn, the schedule included Indicus, Counterpoint, Tsai and Available. Lockie and Cam would probably be done around the same time Greer and I were. There was the hope we could all take a hack in the woods and then go for pizza. Basta wasn't open yet but Diego was there every day preparing and practicing with the staff. Using us as test pigs probably would make him very happy.

I hadn't mentioned this idea to anyone yet. Sometimes it was better to spring it at the last moment, then they couldn't come up with so many excuses to back away. I thought this was what Lockie meant when he kept saying we should go square dancing. Going out once in a while and not thinking about the horses was healthy, rather like a trail ride for humans. We needed to do more of that.

Greer was tucking a stray lock of hair into her hairnet when Eileen Abbott came to the front door.

I greeted her and led Eileen through the house to the kitchen where Jules had placed some shortbread cookies and a large pitcher of iced tea. Eileen commented about how lovely these old farmhouses were and I gave her a very brief history of how long my family had been there. She was surprised, of course. Most of the old farms were in the hands of newcomers, like Victoria.

Greer entered with a swish of fabric and Joly trotting along beside her when there was enough room. We settled ourselves at the table and Jules brought small dishes of lemon mint sorbet she had made that morning.

No one ever left the farm with an empty stomach.

Eileen asked questions between the cookies and sorbet, but it was Greer who drove the interview. She knew exactly what points needed to be stressed. Later on in the day, Greer wasn't going to say "I should have mentioned the clinic!" There was a mental list being followed and it was Eileen's job to keep up.

We finished the interview, and our snack, then went outside where Eileen raved about the view and began taking photos of the vista. I called Cap so she would know we were on the way.

As we were walking to the barn, Parti began walking with us and Eileen seemed somewhat unnerved by his arrival.

"Is this horse supposed to be loose?"

"No, but there's not much we can do about it. He's a real Houdini," I replied and pointed to the construction at the top of the driveway. "That's why we're having the electric gate installed."

"It's my horse," Greer said. "His name is Partial Stranger."

"That's an unusual name," Eileen replied, writing it down in her notebook.

"He was given to me by an unusual person," Greer said.

We arrived at the barn where Cap had Tea tacked and waiting for us.

I felt a tug on my arm that pulled me back into the barn.

"What are you doing down here?" Lockie asked in a low tone.

"Doing the newspaper interview. Why?"

"Tarrant's coming to look at the new horse."

With a glance toward Greer outside, I could see she was being helped onto Tea. "When?"

"Any time now."

"Call and tell him to um…stop at the Grill Girl for one of their great hamburgers."

Cap handed Greer her stag horn hunt whip with the long thong and popper. She was the perfect image of a lady going out with the field.

"That will sound ridiculous," Lockie said.

"What do you think is going to happen if those two run into each other?"

"They'll behave like adults."

I strode away from him before saying anything I would be sorry about later.

And that was just in time to see Mark Kobayashi's expensive foreign car turn onto the driveway. Fortunately or unfortunately there were several trucks in the way at that moment so they had to stop half way. They got out.

Greer looked at me. "Is that who I think it is?"

"Yes, but hang on, Greer. Lady Rowe!" I called after her as Greer started cantering up the driveway.

"What's Gracie doing?" Cam asked.

I started running, seeing Greer pull Tea up and somehow jump off.

Parti, seeing all the fun and wanting to be part of it, started trotting along with me, tail like a flag.

Greer let Tea go and started chasing Tarrant up the driveway, waving her hunt whip at him.

"Get your dirty damn self off my farm!"

"What the hell's the matter with you?" he shouted back.

"You don't have a very good memory!" She swung the whip at him again.

"Are you talking about the night of the Arboretum Ball?" Tarrant was managing to stay just out of range of her whip.

"No, you blinking idiot! Although that's a contributory factor. That's called date rape if you don't know the term."

"You're mad."

Cam and Lockie had arrived and were watching with interest while Parti followed her.

She used her whip again and Tarrant avoided her. "I am! I've been mad for years."

"What did I do?" Tarrant shouted back.

"What did he do?" Cam asked.

"I have no idea," I replied. So far he sounded like a real bugger.

"Accolade? Do you remember him?" Greer chased Tarrant down the driveway and into the carriage house yard.

"Yes." Tarrant vaulted over the fence.

"Good jumper," Lockie commented.

"Cleared it," Cam admitted.

"You beat him until he was bloody! I have a policy. What is done to the horse, should be done to the person. Break out the bandages, Lord High Mucky-Muck because you're getting payback!" Greer ran up the driveway, whip in one hand, holding her skirt up with the other.

Cam ran after her, caught up within a few strides, and put his arms around her so hers were pinned down.

"Let me go!"

"No."

Tarrant stopped and smiled, thinking he was safe.

"Let me show you how to use this whip."

Cam took it from her, brought his arm back in a big arc and flung the whip at Tarrant.

Tarrant scooted away.

Expertly, Cam swung the whip again, it cracked like the report from a gun. Tarrant jumped.

I didn't think the popper touched him but it was very close.

"Needless to say, I'm not buying any horses from this stinking riding academy!" Tarrant ran to the car, and Mark backed out, spinning the tires as they went.

"Sorry," I said to Lockie.

"No problem. He's not our type of clientele."

"What happens to you, Gracie?" Cam asked.

"You're never here!"

Cam thought about that for a moment. "Do you want me to be here?"

Greer looked away.

"You have to say the words. That's how it works."

"If I nod?"

"I'll accept it for now, but that won't get you out of it."

Greer nodded.

Cam smiled. "Okay."

Putting his arms around her, pulling her so close, her body conformed to his, then Cam kissed her.

"That's settled," he said when he let her go.

The End

Join our mailing list and be among the first to know when the next Bittersweet Farm book is released.
Send your email address to:
barbara@barbaramorgenroth.com

Note: All email addresses are strictly confidential and used only to notify of new releases.

WHO'S WHO AT THE FARM

Talia Margolin—18 year old trainer at Bittersweet Farm, her horse is Freudigen Geist, stable name CB, Butch her junior horse and two ponies Garter and Foxy Loxy.

Greer Swope—Talia's 18-year old sister. Her horses are Counterpoint, Citabria whose stable name is Bria and Tea Biscuit her junior hunter.

Andrew Swope—their father

Sarah Margolin—Talia's mother, now deceased, Andrew's ex-wife

Victoria Rowe—Greer's mother, Andrew's ex-wife, lives at Rowe House Farm a few miles away

Julietta "Jules" Finzi—private chef and confidant to the girls.

Lockie Malone—head trainer at the farm, Talia's love interest. His horse is Wingspread.

Cameron Rafferty (Cooper)—show jumper, Greer's potential love interest. His horses are Whiskey Tango, Jetzt Oder Nie and his childhood pony, Remington.

Kate Rafferty Cooper—Cam's mother

Fitch Cooper—Cam's father

Kerwin Rafferty—Cam's grandfather

Caprice "Cap" Rydell—barn manager, her horse is Bijou

Millais "Mill" Crocker—Cap's boyfriend who is involved with the polo horses belonging to Teche Chartier.

Emma Crocker—Mill's younger sister.

Kitty Powell–Friend to Lockie and Cam, from Delaware, who is transitioning to eventing.

Teche Chartier—owns Chartier Spices "Scorching the world one mouth at a time". From Louisiana originally, Teche has a large estate nearby, one in Florida, travels on business and he enjoys life and horses.

Poppy Beck—Talia's riding student. Her pony is Tango Pirate.

Aly Beck—Poppy's mother.

Gincy Hamblett—Talia's riding student. Her pony is Beau Peep.

Annie Zakarian–new student.

Tarrant Heath-British show jumper, family friends of Greer's English side of the family, now living in New York.

Holliday "Day" Jamieson—local rider, her grandmother is the master of the Newbury Hunt. A talented artist, her horse is named Poussiere de Lune, Moon Dust and his stable name is Moonie.

Sibby Jamieson—Master of the Newbury Hounds and Day's grandmother

Mauritz Schenker—Dressage legend teaching out of Balanced Rock Farm.

Dr. Denise Newbold—New vet in the area, amenable to helping Greer get the word out on good horse management.

Diego Morosoli-Owner of the new Italian restaurant in town, Basta.

Ami Gish—young summer student, who fell off and broke her leg.

Paul Gish—Ami's father, who is suing Talia for negligence.

Freddi—working student at Bittersweet

Greg Tolland—Victoria's farm manager, suspended for dicey financial dealings, behaving now. Tracy lives with him.

Tracy Dunham-former working student at Bittersweet, moved to Rowe House Farm to be with Greg Tolland.

Eileen Abbott-Local newspaper reporter

Joly—Greer's rescued pit bull puppy, who adores her

Lord and Lady Rowe–Greer's grandparents

Buckaroo "Buck" Bouley—15 year old who wants to be an event rider

Peter Bouley—Buck's father

Nicole Boisvert—Greer's junior division nemesis. Her new hunter Obilot, was acquired by Bittersweet Farm.

Ellen Berlin—runs the business end of the Miry Brook Hunt Club

Mackay Berlin—Ellen's son. He's a charming financial advisor and helped organize the Miry Brook show.

Fiori "Fifi" Finzi—Jules's beautiful bad girl sister.

Betsey Harrowgate—side-saddle rider from Aside Not Astride.

Nova Reeve—college activist who interviews Greer.

Ethan Monroe—the town police officer married to Sassy. Jingles is their dog.

Jingles—a Mastiff who participates in the Ambassador of Good Cheer project, Greer's charity.

Trish Meade—14 year old girl in the 4-H who trained Oliver to be the Ambassador of Good Cheer.

Oliver—rescue dog who is very cheerful

Joly—Greer's rescued pit bull puppy, who adores her

Dr. Fortier—the veterinarian

Dr. Jarosz—Lockie's medical specialist in New York City.

Amanda Hopkins—teacher who is also helping Greer with her charity work

Bertie Warner—Greer's side saddle instructor

Sloane Radclyffe—wealthy socialite with a large farm in Pennsylvania

Ellis Ferrers—a rider at the farm briefly, and bought a horse through Cam

Jennifer Nicholson—Lockie's ex-girlfriend

Sabine—Greer's former best friend

Rui-their former train-wreck of a trainer

Gesine Hamm-Hartmann—Lockie's dressage trainer in Germany.

THE PONIES

Knock Knock-Dina Gnehmn's trade for Penuche

Penuche-Nice show pony Greg Tolland acquired and gave to Talia

Spindrift-Annie Zakarian's pony

Beau Peep-Gincy Hamblett's pony

Tango Pirate-Poppy Beck's pony

Calling All Comets-Bittersweet Farm's Pony of the Americas.

Foxy Loxy-Talia's pony

Garter-Talia's pony

Remington-Cam's pony

ACKNOWLEDGEMENTS

Much gratitude to the wonderful photographer

Irene Elise Powlick

for the cover photo.

If you're impressed with her work, as I am,

check out her website

www.irenepowlickphoto.weebly.com

About the Author

Barbara got her first horse, Country Squire, when she was eleven years old and considers herself lucky to have spent at least as much time on him as she did in the dirt. Over the years, she showed in equitation classes, hunter classes, went on hunter paces, taught horseback riding at her stable and went fox hunting on an Appaloosa who would jump anything. With her Dutch Warmblood, Barbara began eventing and again found herself on a horse with great patience and who definitely taught her everything important she knows about horses. She now lives with Zig Zag, a Thoroughbred-Oldenburg mare.